ASSASSIN'S WITNESS

OTHER FIVE STAR TITLES BY PAUL COLT

HISTORICAL FICTION

Boots and Saddles: A Call to Glory (2013)
A Question of Bounty: The Shadow of Doubt (2014)
Bounty of Vengeance: Ty's Story (2016)
Bounty of Greed: The Lincoln County War (2017)
Sycamore Promises (2018)
Friends Call Me Bat (2019)
Grasshoppers in Summer (2020)

GREAT WESTERN DETECTIVE LEAGUE

Wanted: Sam Bass (2015)
The Bogus Bondsman (2017)
All That Glitters (2019)

A GREAT WESTERN DETECTIVE LEAGUE CASE

ASSASSIN'S WITNESS

PAUL COLT

FIVE STAR
A part of Gale, a Cengage Company

LIBRARY OF CONGRESS CATALOGING-IN-PUBLICATION DATA

Names: Colt, Paul, author.
Title: Assassin's witness : a Great Western Detective League case / Paul Colt.
Description: First edition. | Waterville, Maine : Five Star Publishing, [2021] | Series: Great Western Detective League
Identifiers: LCCN 2021011537 | ISBN 9781432885991 (hardcover)
Subjects: GSAFD: Western stories.
Classification: LCC PS3603.O4673 A88 2021 | DDC 813/.6—dc23
LC record available at https://lccn.loc.gov/2021011537

First Edition. First Printing: October 2021
Find us on Facebook—https://www.facebook.com/FiveStarCengage
Visit our website—http://www.gale.cengage.com/fivestar
Contact Five Star Publishing at FiveStar@commat;cengage.com

Printed in Mexico
Print Number: 01   Print Year: 2022

ASSASSIN'S WITNESS

PROLOGUE

Yuma Penitentiary
Arizona Territory
1879

The blue uniformed guard led the way through the cellblock, footfalls tapping a hollow tattoo. Barred shadows line concrete walls like hash marks counting the never-ending passage of time. Inmates, sullen and curious, follow the bull and his privileged prisoner through gray-shadowed gloom. They hate the silver haired patrician for the comforts afforded his incarceration. They hate him, but they keep their thoughts to themselves. Prisoner or no, the man is deadly.

Rested and relaxed the Don Victor Carnicero makes this walk for the last time. His appeals have at long last been rewarded by an order for his release. It had proven expensive. Lawyers were only the beginning. The real money paid out in bribes. Shedding himself of these dreary circumstances was more than worth the cost. Clad in his customary white linen he made stark contrast to the coarse striped pajamas worn by the occupants of other cells. He'd chafed at confinement in spite of accommodations that included a comfortably furnished double cell stocked with cigars, tequila, and amenities generally withheld from other inmates. Anything could be had for a price, even in prison. In prison, prices tended to obscene. Obscenity suited a Patrón's position among a penitentiary filled with peons.

The guard led him down the block to a staircase leading to

7

reception. He unlocked the barred door and stepped aside. The Don smiled at his first breath of free air in more than a year. He fingered his neatly trimmed white goatee, Don Victor Carnicero, El Patrón to his El Anillo crime syndicate known as Ring. He carried himself with a proud bearing and an aura of power, suggesting a larger stature than his average height. Handsome still in the echo of vigor, waves of white hair set off a swarthy complexion with the patina of polished leather. He filled the stark expanse of the reception chamber with the presence of a benevolent grandfather were it not for his eyes. Deep set and black they glittered with an inner fire that smoldered in equanimity or flamed in rage. Little ruffled his outward demeanor. Only his eyes gave light to a ruthless hard edge.

He presided over a shadowy network known to the very few. His organization discretely served the indelicate needs of the rich and powerful. His clients included crooked politicians, organized labor, robber baron industrialists, affluent anarchists, and high stakes criminals. El Anillo specialized in murder for hire, protective extortion, and liquidation of illegal merchandise, all performed in a manner designed to strictly assure his client's anonymity as well as his own. All his services came at exorbitant fees as befit the risks he took and his client's means of payment. His recent incarceration resulted from a diamond swindle gone bad, and an unfortunate encounter with operatives of the Great Western Detective League, an encounter he meant to avenge in blood.

Escobar awaited his Patrón beyond the prison gates with a carriage. The man could be counted on to carry out the Don's instructions with meticulous attention. Nothing would stop him. A slender man with a wiry build he moved with the stealth of a scorpion. His features were lean and hard, pockmarked by childhood disease. His left cheek bore the scar of a knife fight that ended the worse for the Indio who cut him. Little was known of him beyond his intense loyalty to the Don. Some speculated privately he might be Patrón's illegitimate son, though any resemblance ended with a violent temper. Ruthless in the extreme, he could be brutally sadistic as he carried out orders without question. Within the Don's inner circle, he was known as El Ejecutor, the enforcer.

The heavy metal doors swung open at precisely twelve o'clock noon. Don Victor stepped into a blazing sun, blinked, and strode to the carriage.

"Patrón," Escobar said.

"My son, it is good to see you in fresh air, free of the stench of that godforsaken hellhole. Come, let us make haste." He climbed into the carriage. Escobar took the driver's seat and collected the reins. He clucked to the team, a pair of matched bays, and set off at a brisk pace to Yuma in time for an eastbound train.

"Were the amenities of your incarceration not of the quality we purchased?"

"The quality was as agreed. No amount of amenity can mask the disgust of penitentiary. Why do you ask, my son?"

"Only if you did not receive the comforts we paid for, I would see to it the warden paid for it with his manhood."

"Let him keep it for now."

The carriage road into town paralleled the railroad tracks baked in blazing sun. Endless sand and scrub spread desert north and south.

"All is in readiness for my arrival?"

Escobar nodded.

"Where have you found a hacienda?"

"El Paso. Near the border. Well hidden."

"Bueno."

CHAPTER ONE

O'Rourke House
Denver
1910

I strolled along a pleasant tree-lined lane on a sunny warm Saturday in May. I found a stately Victorian in the middle of the block, neatly bordered by tended gardens tucked behind a wrought iron fence. A central gate opened to a walkway leading to three steps up to a broad porch fronting the length of the house. Lace-covered leaded glass windows added a welcoming touch to polished wood double doors. I confess to an odd sense of having been here before, though knowing full well I never had. The reason for my sense of premonition should unfold presently.

By way of introduction for those whose acquaintance I have not made before, my name is Robert Brentwood. I beg indulgence of those who may be familiar with this part of the story, but I should explain for the benefit of those new to these adventures. I am employed as a reporter for the *Denver Tribune,* though in this venture I've come to compile the stories of the Great Western Detective League. The idea for this project first occurred to me when I stumbled on reports of this association of law enforcement professionals in the *Tribune* archives. Imagine my surprise when I discovered, quite by accident, the mastermind behind this storied network of crime fighters still alive and comfortably ensconced at the Shady Grove Rest Home

11

and Convalescent Center. My nascent writing career seemed foreordained by the discovery.

As things came to pass, the Colonel, David J. Crook (U.S. Army Ret.), agreed to assist me in my ambition in return for . . . modest compensation. A bottle of contraband whiskey surreptitiously delivered each week at no small risk to my personal happiness. That too shall become apparent presently. In return we completed three stories dramatizing the extraordinary exploits of the Colonel's legendary organization. Well, perhaps not yet legendary; it shall certainly be so before we are finished.

The Colonel and I struck up something of a remarkable relationship over his telling of these tales. Regrettably we lost him to the ravages of age last year. I'll not deny I wept like a child at his passing. He could be curmudgeonly, sarcastic, and an impossible tease. We loved him, my Penny and me. We owed him much.

My Penny is Miss Penny O'Malley. She served as the Colonel's nurse at Shady Grove Rest Home and Convalescent Center. The Colonel took it upon himself to introduce my tongue-tied self to her when I couldn't bring myself to do so. In doing so he imparted an amazing possibility into my life. He did it out of the irascible conviction he might not live long enough to see me speak for myself. That is quintessentially, the Colonel. He was an incorrigible tease who felt perfectly permitted to barge into our private affairs without regard to social convention or the least consideration for proper courtesy. He did of course gain the desired result. My relationship with Penny has grown to the point where I've asked her to marry me and, indeed, she accepted.

When the Colonel passed, I feared through my veil of tears, I might be forced to continue these stories without his guidance. Providence provided at his funeral. An old colleague appeared to pay his respects. I spotted Briscoe Cane at the Colonel's graveside. I didn't know him, but aside from a few years of age he rang true to the Colonel's description. Hickory hard frame of angular construction, features stitched in worn saddle leather. I ventured a speculation.

He's taken up residence here in Denver at this very house. We shall begin anew this very morning. Before we do, I should like you to meet him as the Colonel once introduced him to me. The Colonel recruited him in the matter of a robber fugitive known as Sam Bass. As the Colonel told me of Cane's recruitment, he used his considerable facility with information to impress Cane with what he knew of him.

"I know, for example, you favor a pair of fine-balanced bone-handled blades, one sheathed behind that .44 holster rig and the other in your left boot. I know you can draw and throw with either hand fast enough to silently defeat another man's gun draw.

"I know you are equally fast with that Colt and a .41 caliber Forehand & Wadsworth Bull Dog rigged for cross draw at your back. Some consider a spur trigger pocket pistol the weapon of choice for a whore. Such a notion would sadly misestimate your use of it. Those that do, seldom do so for long.

"I also know you carry a Henry rifle and I'm told you can pluck out a man's eye at a thousand paces. I know that when called for, you possess a master craftsman's skills with explosives. In my humble opinion, were it not for the staunch religious foundation afforded by your upbringing you might have had a more prosperous career as an assassin than the one you have as a bounty hunter."

Cane resisted at first. The Colonel as he soon learned could be quite persuasive. In the end Cane agreed to join the Colonel's Great Western Detective League. I doubt he'd admit it, but I suspect he never looked back.

I rapped the heavy brass door knocker.

A pleasantly attractive older woman responded to my knock. "Yes?"

"Robert Brentwood, madam. I've come to see Mr. Cane."

"Is he expecting you?"

"He is. We met at Colonel Crook's funeral."

"I see. Come in."

The foyer smelled of floor wax with a hint of fresh baked bread.

"Quite a man, Colonel Crook," she said, closing the door. "Did you know him?"

"No. I read the newspaper report of his death. It was quite flattering."

"It was. I wrote it."

She lifted a brow in a second appraisal of me. "You're a newspaper man then?"

"I am."

"Are you doing a story on Briscoe?"

"No, ma'am. I'm hopeful he'll do one for me."

"I'm afraid I don't understand. By the way, I'm Angela Fitzwalter, proprietress of O'Rourke House."

"Pleased to meet you, ma'am. In addition to my newspaper work I write books. I've written three on the exploits of the Great Western Detective League with the Colonel's help. Now I'm hopeful Mr. Cane will help me continue the work. He used to work for the League, you know."

"I did know that. One can scarcely know Briscoe and not. Have a seat in the parlor. I'll call him."

I took a comfortable chair in a handsomely appointed, stiffly formal, Victorian parlor. She climbed the stairs. Presently I overheard.

"Briscoe, you have a caller."

He followed her down the stairs creak by creak. I rose.

"Mr. Cane. Robert Brentwood, we met at Colonel Crook's funeral. I hope you recall."

"Of course, Robert. I'm old, not that old."

"I was hoping to follow up on something you said that day."

"Oh? What is that?"

"I asked whatever happened to Beau Longstreet. You said it's a long story. I thought it might make for an interesting book."

He smiled at some faraway vision. "It is a long story."

"Would you gentlemen care for a cup of coffee?"

"That would be very nice, Angela. As I recall, Robert, you and the Colonel had . . . an arrangement to compensate him for assisting you."

"We did. I thought you might recall that." I reached in my coat pocket and drew out a bottle of Old Crow.

Angela straightened. "You remember the rules, Briscoe. Moderation in strong spirits and I am the judge of moderation."

"Yes, dear."

"And your attempts at fraternization in no way affect my judgment. Now, excuse me while I pour coffee."

I winked. "I didn't mean to cause a problem, Mr. Cane."

"No problem. Those have been house rules going back to Maddie O'Rourke's time. Rules are made to be broken." He glanced toward the kitchen, conspiratorially. "Angela's all right when she lets her hair down. Don't tell her I said so. Her judgment can be affected by a couple fingers of good whiskey." He held up the bottle, "Oh, and please, call me Briscoe."

Angela returned with two steaming cups of coffee. "Call if you need anything." She returned to the kitchen. We took seats. I drew out my notepad and pencil.

"Now about that long story."

"It all started with that railroad dustup over the Royal Gorge right-of-way to the Leadville silver strike. That got El Anillo back in business not long after blind Lady Justice let Don Victor Carnicero out of prison."

CHAPTER TWO

Topeka, Kansas

Stephen Atkins studied the route map, tapping his finger on Leadville, Colorado. The silver strike there promised lucrative rail service. The right-of-way to service Leadville would traverse the chasm known as Royal Gorge. He scanned the report from Atkins, Topeka & Southern General Manager W. B. Strong. It would be one expensive section to build. Trestle track always was expensive and dangerous. The gorge came by its need for trestle honestly. Carved out of granite by the Arkansas River over millions of years, the gorge dropped twelve hundred feet to the riverbed. A mere fifty feet wide at its narrowest point, rail service through the gorge would accommodate but a single section of track. Building a trestle anchored to solid rock of sufficient strength to support the weight of a fully loaded freight train would challenge the engineers who designed it and the lives of those daring enough to build it. For all of that the silver returns would be well worth the cost and risk. Therein might lie opportunity too.

Right-of-way to the Royal Gorge belonged to AT&S's rival, the Denver & Rio Grande Railroad. Atkins's bankers described the D&RG financial condition as "cash strapped." Atkins doubted the D&RG balance sheet would be up to the task of building the section.

"Can you do it, Mr. Strong?"

"The engineering? Sure. If you can finance it, we can build

16

it. What's to be done about the Denver & Rio Grande right-of-way claim?"

"I doubt they can finance it. Palmer needs cash. He may be open to leasing that section to us. You get busy with your crew and material. Leave the D&RG to me."

Denver

W. J. Palmer, President of the Denver & Rio Grande, gazed out his office window to late winter sun glare. The street rutted in icy puddles and muddy snow. A passing wagon splashed mud in its wake. He stared vacantly as he ran through his impending appeal in his mind, rehearsing his arguments point by point. Lenders were in the business of earning returns on risk capital. Silver promised handsome returns. Surely returns worthy of financing a short section of track. Difficult to be sure and expensive by the engineering estimates, but short with lucrative returns to be had from successfully spanning the canyon crossing to Leadville.

"Mr. Cartwright is here."

"Send him in, Vincent."

Jeremiah Cartwright, Esquire, represented the D&RG bondholder syndicate. Tall and impeccably turned out in gray flannel, green silk cravat, gold stick pin with beard, and mustache freshly trimmed, Cartwright cut a sartorial figure.

"Jeramiah, welcome." Palmer extended his hand.

"William."

"Please have a seat. Thank you for coming so promptly."

"My clients have a great deal at stake where the Denver & Rio Grande is concerned. Any matter affecting the service of your indebtedness becomes a matter of interest. As you might imagine, we have some concern at the condition of your finances given the statements we are provided by the banks."

"Yes, well, I believe we are presented with an opportunity to allay any concerns you might have."

Cartwright made a steeple of his fingertips. "I'm listening."

"The silver strike in Leadville promises rich service. Denver & Rio Grande holds right-of-way to Royal Gorge. Develop that section of track and we shall have cash flowing to our coffers in rich measure."

"Happy prospect that. You said develop that section of track. I'm sure you mean trestle track. That represents some serious engineering. Have you a plan?"

Palmer passed the design across his desk. The lawyer fitted wire-rimmed spectacles over his ears and studied the drawing.

"Elaborate."

"Up to bearing the load."

"And a budget?"

Palmer slid a sheet of figures across the desk.

The lawyer glanced at the lower right corner, knit his brow, and met Palmer's eyes.

"I shall have to consult with my clients."

"Of course."

Great Western Detective League Office
Denver

Colonel David J. Crook shook his head and tossed the telegram on his desk. He stepped to the office door. Late afternoon sun painted wood surfaces a warm golden glow.

"Longstreet, Cane, a moment if you please."

Longstreet led the way to the Colonel's office. Tall, muscular, and handsome, Beau Longstreet's family roots ran deep in the old South. He came from the fringes of the more prominent Longstreet line best known for his cousin, the daring general who served under Robert E. Lee. Beau followed the family military tradition in service to the Southern cause without the privilege of West Point education. He parlayed his family name into a junior officer's appointment and rose to the rank of Captain before the cessation of hostilities. Humiliated in defeat, he drifted west, reaching St. Louis penniless. He signed on as a Pinkerton guard out of necessity and soon demonstrated a knack for protection. They'd done a good deal of defending in the later stages of the war. His experience as a field commander soon distinguished his performance for the Pinkerton Agency. He gained greater responsibility in his assignments and as the company followed the railroads and goldfields west so did Beau Longstreet.

A devil-may-care lady's man by nature, on a case he was circumspect, logical, and intuitive. He signed onto General Crook's detective association in Denver after encountering Cane in their pursuit of the notorious train robber Sam Bass. He soon impressed his new employer as a master investigator. Longstreet came in for the tough cases. He had a knack for the subtle clue, the overlooked fact, a cold trail, and the foibles of human nature.

"Something wrong?" he said.

"Not yet. Read this. The warden at Yuma is a friend. I just got this."

"They let him out?" Longstreet handed the telegram to Cane.

"On appeal."

"Appeal to what? The man is guilty as sin."

"Likely on appeal to a judge that could be bought."

"Now what?" Beau said.

"We wait. I'll put the word out to the League to be on the lookout for him. I doubt he'll go back to Santa Fe. His base there is in some state of, shall we say, disrepair courtesy of Briscoe's handiwork there. He'll turn up. When he does, we'll know where to look when he goes back into business."

"You don't think he's reformed then?" Beau said.

19

"Do you?"

O'Rourke House

Shadow blanketed the street at the end of the day as Longstreet made his way home. *Home,* he'd come to think of it as that. Hadn't thought much about home since he left what remained of the plantation at the end of the war. That home left little more than cinders after Sherman passed through. Charred memories didn't invite. Maddie did.

Maddie O'Rourke supported herself in a man's world, operating a boardinghouse. A fine figure of a woman, she had wholesome good looks with waves of auburn hair. Girlish golden freckles splashed lightly across the bridge of an upturned nose, the only flaw to a perfect golden complexion. She spoke the buttery brogue of her immigrant heritage with a merry laugh and deep green eyes cloaked in sobriety but for a hint of merry Irish mischief. In a town starved for female companionship, Maddie O'Rourke stood apart. She had a stubborn independent streak that suited her temperament. The whole of her captivated Longstreet from the moment he'd first taken a room in her house. She made him feel comfortable. He'd had the opposite effect on her at first. He intruded on her self-sufficient sense of well-being. She had no need of the attentions of any man let alone one such as Beau Longstreet. Still, she found him a handsome brute. Charming in his glib way. In time she'd made peace with her demon and welcomed him with her warmth.

The door swung open to the smell of something good coming from the kitchen. He crossed the dining room. She met him in the door to the kitchen. Her eyes smiled. He brushed a flour smudge from her cheek.

"Miss me?"

She answered with her arms.

Home was a kiss. A kiss to give a man longing. Home felt good.

"You know I miss you when you're gone. Why must you persist in asking?"

"Because I like to hear you say you do."

"You are impossible."

"Quite the contrary. I'm eminently possible."

She blushed.

He liked that too.

"Something smells good. What's for supper?"

"Roast beef, Irish potatoes, and blackberry pie for dessert."

"All potatoes are Irish."

"German potato salad most definitely is not."

"I prefer Irish." He kissed her again.

"Shed that coat and tie. Make yourself comfortable. There's sherry on the buffet."

"I'll make that two."

"You'll have me burn supper."

"An Irish lass? I should think you can manage a glass."

CHAPTER THREE

Denver
D&RG Offices

"Mr. Cartwright to see you, sir."

"Show him in, Vincent."

Palmer's aide backed out the office door making way for the lawyer. He left the door ajar that he might hear what transpired.

"Jeramiah," Palmer rose at his desk in greeting. "Please have a seat. I presume your visit means you've had an opportunity to consult with your clients."

"It does." Cartwright took the offered seat. He opened his case and drew out the plans and financials for the Royal Gorge section.

"And?"

"I'm afraid the endeavor is too rich for our undertaking."

"Too rich? I don't understand. The potential returns substantially enhance the financial condition of your current investment."

"Perhaps, so long as the silver find holds. That adds speculative risk to a sizable increase in indebtedness to finance the project. We think a more prudent opportunity exists at much lower risk."

"I'm afraid I don't follow."

"Atkins has an appetite for the Royal Gorge risk. He also has the capital to finance construction. My clients believe your best course of action is to lease the right-of-way to the AT&S. Cash

22

flow from the lease would then serve to strengthen your financial position in relation to your current obligations."

"But lease payments would be trivial in comparison to receipts from serving the Leadville mines."

"Trivial to you, security to us. You're simply in no position to take on sizable increases in indebtedness and risk. My clients are more concerned with preservation of capital and return on their existing exposure. You must understand they are bondholders not shareholders who are compensated for taking risk on a project such as the Royal Gorge spur."

"But what am I to tell my directors?"

"The truth. Denver & Rio Grande cannot afford to develop the Royal Gorge right-of-way. Given the urgency everyone sees in the opportunity, we suggest you contact Atkins straightaway before any slippage in ore production has the potential to diminish the value of the lease."

"But this leaves a fortune on the table, Jeramiah."

"It does, William. Our fortune."

The lawyer departed. Palmer slumped at his desk, head in hands. In the outer office, Vincent sat at his desk, pen in hand. He set ink to paper.

My dear Eli . . .

Denver
Holy Redeemer Episcopal Church
1910

My Penny and I made an appointment to meet Father Taylor the following Saturday morning. We became acquainted with Holy Redeemer over the arrangements for Colonel Crook's funeral. Penny saw it as a fine choice for our wedding. I had to agree. The church made a connection to the Colonel and his hand in our impending union that struck me in keeping with the spirit of his attendance. We'd taken to attending mass there following the Colonel's service with the intent of approaching Father Taylor as parish members in requesting our nuptials be performed there.

I couldn't have been more proud of my Penny that bright spring morning. She took my breath away in a frilly white dress festooned with lace and green ribbon. It put me in mind of a bridal gown before we'd so much as discussed that subject. She composed her pretty lips in the hint of a smile reminiscent of the famous painting Mona Lisa. She wore her dark hair curled short with a ribbon to match those of her dress. Her eyes, soft as melted chocolates filled with caramel, never failed to enchant me. She spoke a velvety voice dipped in butterscotch tinted in Irish brogue. A throaty laugh crinkled the sprinkle of freckles on the bridge of a pixie fine nose. A light scent of vanilla ice cream flavored her presence as we climbed the steps to the church.

Inside the church bright sunshine muted to a sepia glow. Our eyes adjusted to the sounds of quiet with scents of furniture polish and candle wax. Father Taylor waited for us at the altar. We made our way up the aisle, Penny on my arm, ceremony in the moment. Father Taylor smiled.

"A lovely couple on a lovely day. Have a seat." He signaled the front pew. "Now what may God's church do for you?" He asked with a knowing wink.

"We'd like to discuss the possibility of a wedding."

"Splendid."

At that Penny and Father took over. I drifted along with their conversation satisfied I'd made it this far. I also sensed I floated on a river of preparations that required little more of me than yielding to the current. Unexpectedly I learned we would be given instruction. Penny seemed to understand. It never occurred to me I might not know how to be married, but the church seemed to think otherwise. A bend in the stream. I acquiesced.

Lunch followed our meeting with Father Taylor with our favorite ice cream sundaes for dessert.

"I couldn't help thinking of him as we sat there," I said.

"The Colonel? I felt him too."

"It seems quite right to have him with us as we begin our journey together."

"It does. Will you buy him a drink at the reception?"

"A drink? I'm not sure what you mean."

"Oh, come now, Robert. You know, your little weekly contraband whiskey? Do you really think I didn't know?"

"You did?"

"Of course."

"It was against the rules."

"So it was. Had it become a problem, I'd have been forced to do something about it. The Colonel maintained the soul of discretion. It mellowed his mood and did him no harm. In such circumstances, I reckoned it a rule made to be broken. Will you continue the practice with Mr. Cane?"

I nodded, speechless. Caught red-handed the whole time. I could only imagine the mirth she must have found at our clumsy pretense at skulduggery. I granted her the mirth deserved and loved her for not having us exposed.

O'Rourke House
1910

Lunch generally wasn't included in room and board at O'Rourke House. When it came to Briscoe Cane, Angela made a quiet exception. Sandwiches in a sun-washed kitchen.

"Are you expecting young Brentwood this afternoon?"

"I believe he'll be by."

"Must be time for a refill."

"It is."

"Nice young man, even if he indulges your vices."

"I'm particular about my vices. Nothing beyond the guidance of the Good Book."

"To that, I can attest. More coffee?"

"Please."

She poured. "Writing a book, is he?"

"He is. He's actually written several on the Great Western Detective League with the assistance of Colonel Crook."

"And so now you have become the Colonel's surrogate."

"I suppose I have. Rather harmless way for an old man to unburden himself of his stories."

"Mutually beneficial arrangement."

"Rather like you, having a man like me around."

She rolled her eyes. "I count my blessing every day."

"I should think so."

"Don't overvalue your self-estimation."

"Never do."

"He says."

A knock at the door announced Robert's arrival.

"Get on with your story, while I straighten up here."

Cane rose from the table, rounded behind her chair, bent, and brushed a kiss at her cheek.

"You go on now, and take your familiarities with you!" she said, hiding a smile.

CHAPTER FOUR

Manitou Springs

Eli Chorus favored privacy in an atmosphere of understated opulence. His mansion perched at the crest of a secluded front-range foothill, shrouded in pine forest. An enigmatic recluse, Chorus made his fortune in silver turned to profitable investments in a diverse portfolio. His assets afforded him a comfortable life and amusing opportunities to indulge the whimsy of his personal, social, and political views. In Chorus's estimation an American nation built on a destiny to territorial expansion driven by war mongering and greed must be condemned as manifestly unjust. The country constituted a social order deserving of anarchy, disruption, and dispute, so long as none of this interfered with his personal fortune and comforts.

Now well advanced in his sixties, the years had taken their toll on a man withered and bent. His saddle tan features were lined and spotted by the ravages of age. His hair a wild white mane framed in bushes of muttonchops. His thin lips turned down at the corners suggestive of some demeanor between dyspepsia and displeasure. He might have been taken for the handiwork of an undertaker, were it not for his eyes. Bright dark pits, animated by flame, reflected an inner venom, poisonous to those who opposed him. Those with the temerity to cross his purposes were made to pay ruthless consequences. Wealth entitled him to prerogatives he invoked without hesitation.

Among his many investments he numbered a large block of

Denver & Rio Grande stock. He'd purchased the eyes, ears, and occasional affections of Palmer's assistant to keep him apprised of developments affecting his investment. Vincent's letter posed a serious problem. The bondholders' refusal to finance Royal Gorge development would cost him a bloody fortune. Palmer's plan to lease the right-of-way as a means to buy time until financing could be arranged seemed the last gasp of a desperate strategy. At the very least it would take time. Time Palmer might not have in sufficiency. He let the possibilities play through his fertile mind. Perhaps steps might be taken to slow AT&S development, but how? How indeed? Lips lifted imperceptibly at the corners of his mouth. Yes, indeed, that could do it.

The invitation struck him as unusual. The destination upon arrival, even more curious. He'd nearly failed to find it on the ride down from Denver. The foothill road was ill marked. It wound and switched its way into the foothills through pine forest and rock falls before unexpectedly spilling onto a well-hidden plateau. Paddy O'Cairn hauled lines on his rented carriage and stared in awe. He wasn't often summoned to mansions in the middle of nowhere in his capacity as a Knights of Labor union organizer. Who the hell was Eli Chorus and what could he possibly want with the Knights? He'd find out soon enough. He clucked the bay into a brisk trot up the winding drive across the plateau and stepped down from the driver's seat. He dropped the tie-down weight and climbed three steps to a broad veranda. He rapped a heavy brass knocker to stout oaken double doors.

The doors swung open to a giant of a brute costumed in a too tight fitting, starched white coat, strained to contain a barreled bare chest. Ruggedly handsome and wiry tough, O'Cairn didn't intimidate. Nonetheless he was dwarfed by the imposing presence framed in the entry arch.

"Paddy O'Cairn. Mr. Chorus is expecting me."

The brute nodded, stepped aside, and closed the door after O'Cairn. The spacious foyer gave off a muted mahogany glow. The brute led the way down a long dark polished wood corridor to a second set of double doors opening onto a formal parlor.

"Mr. O'Cairn is here, sir."

The old man dressed in a velvet jacket inspected his guest.

"That will be all for now, Cyril."

The behemoth disappeared soundlessly.

"Have a seat, Mr. O'Cairn." A gnarled claw gestured to a wing chair opposite a second.

O'Cairn obeyed. "If I might ask, sir, why am I here?"

"Why do you suppose a man summons a union organizer?"

"You don't look like the union type."

"Looks can be deceiving. As it happens, I find myself in need of just that."

"A union."

"Not merely a union, a union on strike."

"The Knights organize for wages and working conditions. Strikes are a method of last resort."

"Not this time, I'm afraid." Chorus made a temple of crooked fingers in quiet contemplation. "You see in this case your demands must fall on deaf ears, forcing you to strike within the matter of a few weeks."

"How do you know?"

"I know because that is what I am paying you to do. I'm paying you to lead a strike, a nasty, violent strike."

"A strike against who?"

"The Atkins, Topeka & Southern railroad."

"If wages and working conditions are . . . beyond reach, what is the purpose of this strike?"

"You are to disrupt development of the Royal Gorge right-of-way."

"Passage to Leadville and the silver deposits there."

"Very good, Mr. O'Cairn. I see you are current in your thinking. Now can you do it?"

"If the price is right."

"Oh, the price is right. Twenty-five thousand dollars, half now and half in three months if development remains at a standstill."

O'Cairn smiled.

"Splendid."

El Paso

The eastbound Texas & Pacific braked to a screeching steel stop, belching gouts of steam. A faultless blue sky greeted the detraining passengers with a blast of gusty Texas heat. Don Victor stepped down to the platform followed by Escobar. A carriage waited beside the station, its peon driver hat in hand at the arrival of his Patrón. They climbed into the carriage. The driver took his seat.

"Vamanos, Ramon," Escobar said.

The carriage wheeled away from the station, picking up a smart trot into the hill country. Scrub and sand promised little until the carriage began to climb. The driver slowed to turn into the mouth of a narrow defile, barely wide enough for the carriage to pass. A narrow trail snaked its way up and around rock strewn terrain until the trail flattened out atop a low flat mesa, well hidden from the main trail through the hills. There, a low stone hacienda rambled along the base of a hill nearly indistinguishable from the rock formations that concealed it.

The Don surveyed the scene. "You have done well, my son. How did you find such a place?"

"Ramon, the driver, worked for the former owner."

"And you were able to convince him to sell?"

"No. He merely stopped resisting."

"What do you mean he stopped resisting?"

"Where he rests now, he has no need of a hacienda."

"I see. Can this Ramon be trusted with such a secret?"

"He is mute. He considers me his liberator from a former life of servitude."

The carriage drew a halt in a plaza fronting the entrance.

"Come inside, Patrón. See that the accommodations meet with your approval."

Heavy oak doors opened to a cool tiled reception area. A wide corridor served the west wing on the left. A generous parlor with floor to ceiling fireplace sprawled to the right. A formal dining area disappeared in blue shadow beyond the parlor. A second corridor stretched to the back of the hacienda with its kitchen and servants' quarters. The west wing contained a spacious library with double doors leading to a broad veranda with a lovely mountain view. Further down the west corridor, a cluster of generous sleeping chambers completed the floor plan.

Don Victor approved with a nod. Much improved over a Yuma Prison accommodation.

Great Western Detective League Offices
Denver

The freckle-faced kid who ran telegrams for Western Union propped his velocipede against the gaslight post in front of the office and hopped up the boardwalk. His overalls and tattered straw hat looked out of place as he handed Colonel Crook his telegram. Crook pitched the boy a quarter. He caught it midair and was gone.

Longstreet and Cane looked on from their desks as the Colonel tore open the wire. Telegrams had a way of signaling some new development for the League. This one proved no exception.

"He's landed," Crook said.

He registered without need of further inquiry.

"Where?" Longstreet said.

"Sheriff Rojas spotted him arriving in El Paso. He's staying in a mountain hideaway in the hill country."

"Any report of unusual activity?" Cane said.

"Not yet. Considering who we're dealing with, I don't expect we'll have long to wait."

"How do we play it?"

"Sheriff Rojas can't spare a man to watch the place. Might be worth your going down there to have a look, Briscoe. Beau can relieve you in a couple of weeks unless you can work out some more permanent arrangement with the sheriff."

"I'll catch the morning stage."

CHAPTER FIVE

Denver
1910

I soon discovered the complexities of planning a wedding. I'd never thought about such things, which didn't surprise me for having never been married. Of course, neither had my Penny, but she seemed to instinctively know the myriad details that must be considered and arranged in exactly the appropriate manner. I'm quite sure it is a woman thing. My part in most of these choices consisted of listening intently and nodding agreement when called upon to do so. My married friends at the *Tribune* assured me this was good practice for my impending matrimonial state. "Preparation" they said. Rather like the instructions supplied by our weekly visits with Father Taylor. It occurred to me there might be more to married life than matrimonial bliss.

At last we came upon one wedding arrangement in which I had no part, the dress. I was greatly relieved by that. The sheer anxiety of the decision seemed unbearable for my Penny. I should have felt hopelessly out of place and inept in the face of it. The dress had to be perfect, but with so many choices, who could recognize perfection? My Penny struggled. I grieved for her. I assured her whatever dress she chose would be perfect on her. My compassion afforded no consolation. My humble opinion of perfection simply could not be relied upon. The guests, more particularly the women guests, must render true judgment as to perfection. Who knew what they might think? It added up to an endless round of shopping, patterns, and catalogs, exhausting it seemed the very limits of mercantile possibility. I counted my blessings for a visit with Cane.

O'Rourke House

Angela showed me to the parlor.

"Have you brought him another?"

"Another?"

"Bottle."

"I have."

"Is that to be his weekly compensation?"

"It was my practice with the Colonel. Mr. Cane seemed to appreciate that when we discussed it at the funeral."

"I'm surprised Shady Grove permitted it."

"They . . . didn't . . . exactly."

"You circumvented the rules."

I studied the carpet guiltily.

"We have rules of moderation here too you know."

"Oh, Angela, stop browbeating the young man with your prudence. You've been known to imbibe a dram yourself as I've witnessed."

Cane arrived in the nick of time to spare me further discomfit.

"I merely sought to make clear the policy of our house."

"And you've done so to admirable effect, my dear."

"Your dear, I declare. The presumption of your unwelcome attentions."

"Unwelcome?"

She pulled a mask of exasperation punctuated with a foot stomp.

"Of that I am sure. And as to house rules of moderation, I haven't a shadow of doubt as to the nature of your well-made intentions. Good afternoon, Robert."

34

I smiled my greeting and thanks.

"How are the wedding plans progressing?" she asked.

"We've arrived at the matter of choosing a gown. Gratefully I have no part in it."

"Rightfully so. Bad luck for the groom to see a bride in her dress before the wedding."

"So I'm told. I had no idea the decision could be so painful."

"Can't be helped. Most important choice a bride makes."

"Hear that, Robert? More important than consenting to your proposal."

"Don't be silly, Briscoe. You know perfectly well what I mean."

"Perfectly?"

"Perhaps not then, as you've never committed matrimony. I shall endeavor to further your understanding. A bride's dress sets the tone for her most special day."

"Tone? Isn't that task reserved to the organist?"

I sensed Mr. Cane's ability to antagonize his lady with surgical precision.

She rolled her eyes. "Utterly impossible." Lifting a final imperious brow, she turned on her heel and flounced away to the kitchen.

"She knows better than impossible, but we shall indulge her pique. In a curious way, it becomes her. Now where were we, Robert?"

He held out his hand for the bottle. I consulted my notes.

"Denver & Rio Grande bondholders forced Palmer to lease the Royal Gorge right-of-way to Atkins's AT&S."

Topeka

Stephen Atkins sat at his desk, poring over engineering estimates for the Royal Gorge spur, bathed in the tawny golden glow of polished wood. He fully expected to enjoy his next meeting. What could be more delicious than a man's competitor come crawling with hand out and nary a shred of bargaining power.

A tap at the door. "Mr. Palmer to see you, sir."

Atkins set aside his estimates. He smiled.

"Send him in, Mason."

The assistant stepped aside, allowing William Palmer to enter. The door closed behind him. Atkins rose.

"William, welcome." He extended his hand.

"Stephen, you're looking well."

"Please, have a seat."

"Thank you."

"Cigar?"

"Perhaps later."

"To the point then. Your cable mentioned discussing the Royal Gorge."

"It did. I'm prepared to lease the right-of-way for development."

"I must say I'm somewhat surprised given the value of that section. Then I've seen some engineering preliminaries. It looks like expensive construction."

"It is. Given time I'm sure I could arrange the necessary financing, but there is an urgency to establishing service to Leadville."

"And so necessity mothers opportunity."

"I suppose it does. I'm prepared to let you have it for three thousand a month. I make it a fair price in return for the opportunity it affords."

"Yes, I'm sure you see it that way. I, on the other hand, have a somewhat different view. I've taken the liberty of having our attorneys draw a lease at eight hundred a month."

Palmer gaped. "You can't be serious. That section is worth ten times that amount."

"Developed, perhaps so. As is, it's worth a thirty percent reduction in liquidity risk to the interest payments due your bondholders. That is what you truly need, William. Take it or leave it."

Palmer clenched his jaw; red heat rose behind his ears. If being bested by his creditors weren't bad enough, he was now expected to suffer the ignominy of robbery at the hands of his rival. Atkins had all the cards and he knew it. For the moment the D&RG had run out of options.

Pueblo, Colorado

Paddy O'Cairn swept the smoke-filled room with his eyes. Hard men. Calloused hands. Dirt-encrusted bearded faces. Shabbily clothed. This was his moment. The beginning. This time he'd been handed a tool so strong he couldn't believe his good fortune. He always had wages and working conditions to rally them around. This time he had another consideration so compelling, so powerful, as to make organization a foregone conclusion before it could so much as begin. He raised his hands, calling for quiet. The din subsided.

"Men of the Atkins, Topeka & Southern, thank you for coming this evening. You've put in another long hard day in an endless succession of long hard days. I will keep this brief. I have spoken with many of you concerning the organization of a union. None of us have the voice to bargain improvements in wages or working conditions. We know that. But collectively, organized as one voice, we can bargain wages and working conditions. This railroad cannot build itself. The sweat of our labors is needed. In turn for those labors, we should be treated humanely and paid a fair wage." Murmurs of agreement rippled through the crowd.

"The powers behind this railroad will hear our demands only when we make them united in union. And now comes the time we most need to stand together. I am told AT&S has obtained right-of-way to the Royal Gorge. The long days needed to build

that spur will be days fraught with hazard to life and limb.
Today we poured out our labors in sweat. In the gorge some
may pour out their labors in blood. The Royal Gorge represents
a fine prize for the taskmaster, but what does it do for you? It
does nothing more than add danger to the burden of your
labors. You will purchase their prize by your sweat and blood. If
we are to face the dangers of this spur, it must be at a wage
fairly scaled to the risk. What say you to your reward? Are you
with me?"

The room exploded.

"Aye!"

"Aye for union!"

"No blood for these wages!"

He let them have their time. Then raised his hands, holding a
sheet of paper until silence restored.

"Every man here who's with me. Every man here who's for
union, sign your name or make your mark for the Knights of
Labor. With your union, the Knights will put forth your demands."

They came forward one and all.

CHAPTER SIX

Topeka

Lamplight spilled across the desk, creating an island of light amid burnished dark wood. Two large windows behind the desk stood black against a night sky studded in diamonds. Stephen Atkins poured two measures of fine bourbon from a cut crystal decanter into matching glasses. He replaced the bottle on the sideboard and handed a glass to his general manager, W. B. Strong.

"Cigar?"

Strong nodded, selecting one from the offered humidor. Matches flared. Smoke billowed. Bourbon swirled amber light and comforting aroma.

"Excellent." Atkins approved his first sip. "Now, Bill, tell me, how are we progressing with the Royal Gorge crossing?"

"Timber preparation progresses apace. We lack sufficient rope of adequate tensile strength for the rigging. We expect further shipment of that presently. We've offered a wage premium to the crew for those willing to undertake work in the rigging."

"And how is that progressing?"

Strong paused, choosing his words. "Not as many takers there as we'd prefer. It's chancy work."

"Perhaps a slightly higher premium might help."

"It may, though Chief Engineer Corbett believes we may face something of a rather different challenge."

"Oh? And what, pray tell, might that be?"

"Rumor has it the Knights of Labor may be championing formation of a union."

Atkins studied the ash at the tip of his cigar. "The Knights, is it. How credible are these rumors?"

"Credible enough Corbett saw fit to bring it to my attention."

"If the rumors prove true, they could indeed cause us a problem."

"If the men expect an increase in wages in settlement of a labor dispute, that would of necessity increase the premium for rigging work."

"I see. The Knights of Labor . . ." Atkins flicked his ash and drew a smoke in thought. "Curious."

"Curious?"

"The timing. So soon after we obtain right-of-way." He drummed his fingers on the side table in thought. "All right, here's what I want you to do. Notify Pinkerton. We may need their assistance should the situation become . . . unpleasant. I have a hunch there is more to this than coincidence in timing."

"Very good, sir." Strong drained his glass, his business concluded.

El Capitán, though few knew him as that, answered his client's summons. Stephen Atkins knew him only as Esteban, one of a number of identities he might guise himself in where discretion and anonymity were necessitated. Tall and dark, his Spanish bloodlines afforded swarthy good looks. A thick crown of black ringlets framed slate gray eyes, and a pencil thin mustache lined a hard thin upper lip softened below to a look ladies found fetching. He wore a short waist jacket of Mexican cut over a pair of shoulder-rigged, pearl-handled Colts. Close fit riding pants tucked in silver spurred high boots. He entered the office silver-trimmed sombrero in hand. Atkins glanced up at his desk and waved him to a side chair.

"I have reason to believe the Knights of Labor may be attempting to organize a union among my work crews in Pueblo. I need to know if this is true and if it is, who is behind it."

"The first should be easy enough. The second, more difficult perhaps."

"Of that I have my suspicions."

"Who is it you suspect?"

"It is only my suspicion."

"It may help if I know what I am looking for, señor."

"Eli Chorus."

"I know this name. Why do you suspect him?"

"His stock holdings in the Denver & Rio Grande are motive enough to delay extending our service through Royal Gorge. Why the Knights of Labor? Why now? I need answers."

"Sí, señor."

Denver
Pinkerton Office

Little about Reginald Kingsley spoke of a Pinkerton operative, much less master detective. He had the pinched appearance of a librarian or college professor with alert blue eyes, aquiline features, and a full mustache tinged in the barest hint of gray. He favored wool jackets in subdued hues of herringbone or tweed. When called for, he topped himself off in a stylish bowler, properly square to his head, now hung on a coat tree along with an umbrella at the corner of his spacious office. A silver-tipped cane leaned against the corner below. He carried the cane when called for. He might wield it as a baton or break it into a rapier-like blade. In the field, he armed himself with a short barreled .44 Colt pocket pistol cradled in a shoulder holster. He could disappear in a crowd, or turn himself out in a chameleon of disguise to suit his purpose. He dripped comfortable British charm, easily insinuating himself into the trust of the unsuspecting criminal or soon to be informant. This morning he drummed his fingers on a telegram from the head office in Chicago. He disliked rough stuff when it could be avoided, preferring to rely on wit over brawn. This had the unfortunate odor of the latter.

He stepped to the office door. "Trevor, a moment please."

An alert young man looked up from his desk. He followed Kingsley's summons up the aisle between desks. Tall and lean, he moved with the fluid grace of an athlete. Dark wavy hair, deep brown eyes, and crisply hewn features gave Trevor Trevane a rakishly handsome appearance. He possessed a keen mind, naturally suited to investigative work, with a ruthless streak that tended to violent when called for.

"Sir?"

"Have a seat." Kingsley slid the telegram across the desk.

"Labor trouble. Not exactly our cup of tea," Trevane said.

"No it's not. If need be, we'll have to call in Chicago muscle. For the moment we need to get a handle on the situation. I want you to go to Pueblo and have a look around. Figure out what precautions we may need and let me know how the client wishes to proceed."

"I'm on my way."

Pueblo

Trevane found the AT&S offices on a bright, hot, and breezy afternoon. They were housed in a modified passenger car drawn off on a siding near end of track. Renovation rendered it an efficient workspace with a sleeping compartment at the head of the car for the chief engineer. Trevane climbed the rear platform and entered the office. A distinguished gentleman in a black frock coat with white mustache and bushy muttonchops hunched over an expansive desk cluttered with engineering drawings. A weather-featured man in overhauls with a square jaw and handlebar mustache stood at his side. The senior man looked up.

"May I help you?"

"Trevor Trevane, Pinkerton Agency." He proffered his card.

"Ah, yes, we've been expecting you." The man offered his hand. "W. B. Strong, general manager. This is Chief Engineer Robert Corbett." Corbett nodded.

"Pleased to meet you both. What can you tell me about your labor troubles?"

Strong looked to Corbett.

"We believe the Knights of Labor are preparing to organize a union. That, of course, would come with wage and working condition demands."

"Demands we are unlikely to accept," Strong said.

"Resulting in a strike," Trevane said.

"Likely so," Corbett said.

"How would you like to proceed, Mr. Trevane?" Strong asked.

"I'll start by having a look around. See if I can confirm your suspicions. You expect your crew will be receptive to unionization?"

"I'm afraid so," Strong said. "We are about to begin construction of a section, spanning the Royal Gorge to Leadville. The silver strike there represents an important piece of business to our line. I'm sure the urgency of the opportunity is not lost on the Knights. Constructing the trestle will be hazardous work. A consideration they can use to incite the men and increase their demands."

"Curious the timing, don't you think?"

"We do. It begs the question, could someone be deliberately acting to undermine our progress?"

"We've experience in such matters at Pinkerton. We'll see if we can shed some light on all of this for you."

"Of course. Which is why Mr. Atkins insisted we contact your agency to make preparations."

"I understand. We appreciate your confidence. We will make every effort to see that your interests are protected. It's the Pinkerton way."

"Let us know what you find and what measures you deem prudent."

CHAPTER SEVEN

Trevane checked into the Barclay House hotel and changed his suit for workman's dungarees. He made it out to end of track as the men finished up for the day. They shuffled along following the dusty track bed back to town. Most crowded into the Silver Spike Saloon for a beer. Trevane followed. He found a spot at the end of the bar, ordered a beer, and listened. He didn't hear much of anything special until the batwings swung open to a wiry dark-eyed young man. A murmur rippled through the crowd. The young man smiled and made his way to the bar, surrounded by a curious crowd of AT&S men.

Trevane signaled the bartender for another beer.

"Who is that?" He asked the bartender with a lift of his chin to the new arrival.

The bartender set down a frosty stein. "Paddy O'Cairn. He's the union man."

"Obliged."

Trevane moved down the bar to have a listen.

"All I need are these cards," O'Cairn said. "Sign them or make your mark with a witness. Return the cards to me. When we have a majority, I will notify management and put your demands forward from there."

Trevane watched the men pass the cards around the bar. Names were signed, marks made and witnessed. There seemed no hesitation he could observe. O'Cairn waited with his beer for the cards to return. *It won't be long now.* To that thought he added, *And this organizer may know the answers to who and why now.*

Strong inspected the white ash at the tip of his cigar as Trevane took his seat across the desk. Evening shadow darkened the windows reflecting lamplight pooling on the desk.

"What did you find out?"

"They are definitely organizing. The Knight's man is one Paddy O'Cairn. Know him?"

Strong shook his head.

"He passed out voting cards in the Silver Spike earlier this evening. By the look of it, he'll have all he needs soon enough."

Strong gazed at his reflection in the car window through a cloud of smoke. "Did you get any idea of who might be behind this and why?"

"No. But I have an idea on how we might. I'll wire my superior. We'll need at least a dozen men in reserve against contingencies."

Strong nodded. "And how do you propose getting at the who and why questions?"

Trevane smiled a conspiratorial gleam in his eye. "A colleague. You'll see."

Denver

Kingsley read the telegram. A twelve-man security detail, we'll need Chicago for that. *And Agent Maples.* Interesting. He would, of course.

Pueblo

Posing as a laborer, Esteban easily identified the union organizer. One of the men said he could be found at the Silver Spike at the end of the day. Esteban waited at the bar when the work crews came in. The saloon filled with the hum of conversation, sweat scent, and a pall of tobacco smoke. Soon after the wiry Irishman took a back-corner table where men approached him to hand over their cards. Esteban watched for a time before approaching the organizer. Hat in hand, he affected his best peon demeanor.

"Pardon, señor. You are the man of the union, sí?"

The Irishman eyed him suspiciously. The man struck him as too tall and fine featured for an Indio. "I am."

"I am new. I am told I must see you about joining the union."

O'Cairn handed him a card. "Sign or make your mark here."

"What is this?"

"It says you authorize the Knights of Labor to represent you in matters of wages and working conditions. All the AT&S men are signing."

"I have heard of these Knights of Labor. What brings you to Pueblo now?"

"It is time for proper representation."

"Who says this?"

"You ask a lot of questions."

"Only to know if I might be fired."

"You won't be fired."

"How do you know?"

"Powerful people want these men represented."

"Who are these people?"

"People who seek justice for the working man."

"Such justice must be expensive."

O'Cairn knit his brow. "Sign the card."

Topeka

People who seek justice for the working man.

Atkins tapped the telegram on his desk. *Eli Chorus.* It has to be. *What is to be done about the meddlesome old fool?* Labor unrest was doubtlessly cheaper and less risky than advancing Palmer the money to lay track in the gorge. *Cheaper to Chorus. Expensive for me.* He scribbled Esteban his further instructions.

Pueblo

The crowd filled the Silver Spike with boisterous anticipation lubricated by whiskey and beer. Esteban observed quietly from one corner. Trevane watched from another, each man anonymous to the other. Dirty yellow lamplight cast a smoky haze over the assembly. At length, O'Cairn arrived. He elbowed his way to the bar and climbed up on top to be seen and heard. He held up his hands, one clutching a thick stack of union cards.

"Lads!" He appealed for quiet. "Lads!"

The din subsided.

"Lads, we have the votes!"

The room exploded in cheers. O'Cairn let them have their celebration. As it passed, they turned back to hear more.

"We have the votes and we have your demands. First, a ten percent increase in wages."

The men roared their approval.

"Now to this trestle. It will be dangerous work for those who choose to do it. We say nay to the twenty percent premium management offers. We demand for you fifty percent premium for this work!"

The room erupted once again in shouts and cheers.

Esteban, in one corner, could all but hear Atkins from here.

Trevane, in another, wondered if a dozen men would be enough.

O'Cairn raised his hands once again. "Very soon I will present your demands. We will give management thirty days to meet them. If they do not, we need your support for a strike. Are you with me, lads?"

The roar echoed down the track into the gorge.

★ ★ ★ ★ ★

Chief Engineer Corbett hunched over his drawing. Load estimates could be tricky. Misestimate too lightly and the result could be disastrous. Estimate too heavily and unnecessary cost would be incurred. A boot scraped on the step to the car entrance. He glanced up not expecting a visitor. The dark-eyed stranger he'd seen nosing about stepped into the car.

"Mr. Corbett?"

"I am."

The man dropped a stack of cards on his desk. "My name is Paddy O'Cairn, Knights of Labor. We now represent the union organized by your crew."

Corbett eyed the stack of cards.

O'Cairn drew a folded sheet from his coat pocket and laid it next to the cards.

"A list of our demands. You have thirty days to accept them or we are authorized to strike. I have a room at the Silver Spike. You can find me there." He turned on his heel and left.

CHAPTER EIGHT

Denver
1910

So many decisions went into this wedding planning business I lost count. What hadn't escaped me is the realization I was ill-suited to most of them. The decision to propose to my Penny had come easily by comparison, though I recall having agonized over it at the time. After that? I fret over choosing the proper ring. I remembered fondly seeking the Colonel's advice. He'd been willing, but no better suited to the task than I. Eventually I'd dragged myself over that finish line. After that the decisions came fast and furiously. My Penny seemed more than capable of handling them. Still, even she worried over making choices. Then of course I was expected to render an opinion on things over which I had no earthly idea what to consider. Take this morning for example.

We visited a printer for the purpose of choosing wedding invitations. The printer showed us to a round table covered in fat books filled with samples affixed to the pages. Who could imagine the variety of papers, cards, envelopes, and reply cards with little envelopes to put them in? If that weren't sufficiently confusing there were choices as to the type font and the manner of printing. What happened to ink and paper? I shuddered to think what might ensue should two newspapers consider to wed. We paged and paged. My eyes glazed.

"What do you think of this one, Robert?"

"That's very nice."

"Don't you think it too formal?"

"Hmm." *Too formal? What could possibly render a printed card too formal?*

"Oh, look at this one. The cream color is nice, don't you think?"

"I do."

"Though I fear this linen finish may smudge in the post."

Smudge?

She paged and paged.

"Ugh! Look at that. Simply hideous, don't you think?"

"Hideous." In the matter of wedding invitations, it appeared one person's hideous might be another person's perfection. I glanced at my watch. Briscoe was expecting me. I could see this continuing for some time. Perhaps I thought I might move things along.

"Now, there's a dandy," I said.

"Dandy? You can't be serious. Tastefully elegant is what we are after." She paged.

"Tastefully elegant." *I should have known. Whatever constitutes tasteful elegance in printing? I'm a newspaperman. Newsprint, block type, and ink is all I know.* I was pretty sure those choices did not constitute tasteful elegance.

She paged. "Now there's a possibility."

"Nothing could possibly say tasteful elegance any more so."

"It might be a bit pretentious though, don't you think?"

My hopes dashed. "Perhaps just a mite."

She marked the page. A hopeful sign. And paged on.

"I have an idea," I said. "Briscoe is expecting me this afternoon. Why don't you find a few that appeal to you and we can come back next Saturday and you can show them to me."

"You're not interested, are you? It's our wedding and you have better things to do."

"No, no. I swear. Nothing of the sort. It's just that you have some idea of what we are looking for and I don't seem to be much help."

She furrowed her brow. "Oh, very well. Go if you must. I shall simply soldier on by myself."

"I'll pick you up at six for supper and the moving picture show." I kissed her cheek and made a relieved if awkward exit.

Angela responded to my knock at the door. She admitted me with a welcoming smile.

"Robert, so nice to see you. Briscoe is expecting you."

"Thank you. I'm afraid I'm a little late. I was delayed at the printer."

"Printer?" She led me into the parlor.

"Printer?" Briscoe said. "I thought you'd already done the Bogus Bondsman case."

"I have. Sorry I'm late. No, Penny and I were at the printer to choose wedding invitations."

"Ah, how exciting," Angela said.

"I'm afraid I'm not very good at it to the disappointment of my dearest Penny."

"Don't feel bad, son. I doubt I'd be any good at it either."

"Of course you wouldn't, Briscoe. What man would? You don't need to be good at it, Robert, dear. You've only to be interested and agreeable to her selections."

"I'm sure I could manage that, if only she'd make a selection I could agree to. They have books and books of choices on which I am to have an opinion. I sampled a wide range of opinions. None of them proved correct."

"Oh, I shouldn't fret over that if I were you."

"You wouldn't?"

"Heavens no. You're not wrong. It's only your Penny hasn't decided for herself as yet what she wants."

"She says she wants tasteful elegance. I have no idea what that means."

"Of course you don't. Neither does she. Tasteful elegance could mean a great many things depending on a person's taste for elegance. She will know what it means to her when she sees it."

"If she doesn't know what it means until she sees it, how can I possibly have a useful opinion on such an ephemeral notion?"

"Your expressions of opinion show your interest, and even though she may reject them you help her form her own opinion. You've only to be patient until the moment of truth arrives."

"Patient and late. Moment of truth. Thank you for clearing that up for me, I think. Perhaps we should get on with the story, Mr. Cane. I still know something of writing, I think."

CHAPTER NINE

Manitou Springs

The massive door swung open. The brute, Cyril, filled the door-frame. He acknowledged O'Cairn with a grunt. He stepped back, admitting the organizer, closed the door, and led the way down a dimly lit paneled corridor to his master's study. Double doors opened to a large sunlit room paneled in more dark wood lined with bookshelves. A stunning polished carved wooden desk dominated the center of the room, reducing the man seated behind it to diminution. Two plush wing chairs in copper-hued leather were drawn up before the desk.

"Mr. O'Cairn, sir."

Chorus waved O'Cairn in. "Have a seat." He gestured to a wing chair across the desk beside a fieldstone fireplace, rising from hearth to ceiling. "Coffee?"

"Tea, if you please."

"A cup of tea for our guest, Cyril."

The brute backed out of the room.

"Now then, what have you for me?" The financier clasped his hands across his paunch.

"All is in readiness. The union is organized, recognized, demands have been delivered."

"And the demands are?"

"A ten percent wage increase across the board with a fifty percent premium for trestle work. Management has until the end of the month to accept them."

Cyril arrived with a steaming cup of tea and fresh coffee.

Chorus pressed his fingertips to a steeple, squinting into some middle distance.

"Atkins will never agree to those demands."

O'Cairn took a sip of tea and shrugged. "Then we strike."

"And in that you would . . ."

"Stop work and picket the job site until our demands are met."

"Don't you suppose Atkins will take, shall we say, counter-measures?"

"I expect he will call in Pinkerton."

"And?"

O'Cairn lifted a brow with a dark smile. "We shall meet the use of force in kind. Regrettably, violence may entail damage to the job site. Unfortunate, as that may add further delay to the strike."

"Unfortunate, indeed." Chorus clapped his hands with a crooked smile.

Interesting. Esteban watched and waited in the woods east of Chorus's estate. He'd maintained surveillance on the union organizer just as Atkins had instructed. The trail led him here. What could a reclusive financier possibly have to do with a union organizer that did not agree with Atkins's suspicion? And this union organizer no less. What might Atkins make of this? What might he do? For the moment Esteban could guess. He'd not let that last long.

El Paso

Cane stepped off the stage and stretched his aches after a long dusty ride. It felt good to be relieved of the horsehair-hide torture rack that passed for a seat. He could ignore the hot dry wind for the relief it bargained. He waited for his bag on the boardwalk, claimed it as the driver hauled it out of the boot, and headed up the street to the sheriff's office.

Sheriff Pablo Rojas broke out a welcoming grin at his desk when Cane swung through the door.

"Briscoe, mi amigo." He rose, offering his hand. "I thought the Colonel might send you to look in on our friend."

"Pablo, good to see you."

"It's been awhile since we put El Anillo out of the bond business the last time."

"It has. That one didn't even slow them down. When we got the Don in the diamond swindle, I thought we might have put him out of business for a good long time."

"When I heard about it, I thought as much too. What happened?"

"Good lawyers happened. Good lawyers and a sympathetic judge."

"Ah, sí. I know these sympathetic judges. They are the ones with the greasy palms, no?"

"They are. So where is our boy hanging his hat these days?"

"In the hill country northwest of town. I will show you tomorrow. It is not easy to find."

"I'm sure it isn't," Cane said remembering El Anillo's Santa Fe lair.

"Settle yourself at the hotel. They can arrange a horse for you with the livery and I'll take you out there in the morning."

"Much obliged. Stop by the hotel later. I'll buy you a drink and we can have some supper."

"Bueno."

Sunrise turned the sky pink and purple, warming their backs as Cane and Sheriff Rojas rode out stirrup to stirrup at daybreak. Scrub and sand offered little as they climbed into the hills, following a narrow, rutted trail. Rojas signaled a halt at the mouth of a narrow defile.

"This where we leave the main trail." He tossed his head to the left to a narrow defile in the rocks, passing to a winding climb.

"I'd have missed this sure. Fits the pattern. His hacienda outside Santa Fe was well concealed and fortified."

"This one does not appear fortified, but it is concealed as you will see."

Rojas led out on a twisting climb through the rocks. Twenty minutes later he again drew a halt.

"This is as far as we ride." He stepped down.

They hid the horses off the trail and crunched up the slope to a crest where the trail flattened out to a broad plateau. A low stone hacienda squat along the base of a distant hill barely visible in the rock formations that surrounded it.

"You could be looking at it and not see it," Cane said.

"From the main trail to the north, you see nothing."

"So, unless you know it's here, it's not. How did it get here and how did the Don come by it?"

"Both good questions, amigo. The Spanish land grant is old. No sale was recorded to convey it to Don Victor, or anyone else for that matter. If it was sold, it was a private sale."

"Or the previous owner suddenly no longer had need of it. Anything is possible where these people are concerned."

"What do you plan to do now?"

"Let the Colonel know what we have here. I suspect he'll want me to keep an eye on him until we find out what he's up to. Have you kept it under surveillance?"

Rojas shook his head. "I have a small office and a big county to cover. I don't have enough deputies to commit one to a 'see what might develop' assignment."

"I understand. Let's head back to town. I've seen enough for now."

CHAPTER TEN

Denver

The wire came in overnight and was delivered at the office opening. Crook read Cane's telegram at his office door silhouetted in bright sunlight.

"Beau." He waved the foolscap.

Longstreet left his desk. "What's up?"

Crook handed him the wire.

"Now what?"

"The sheriff can't keep an eye on things. My gut says the Don is up to something, or soon will be. One thing we know about these people is they play big and they play for keeps. I'm going to ask Briscoe to stay down there and keep an eye on things for a while. You may have to relieve him in a couple of weeks. I don't know what else to do."

"Given everything we know about El Anillo, I doubt we'll have to wait long."

O'Rourke House

The parlor lamp trimmed low. Sherry caught an amber glow as the evening settled into familiar comfort at the end of a long day. Side by side on the settee, Maddie rested her head on Beau's shoulder.

"Kind of nice, having you around for a few days," she purred.

"Only 'kind of'?"

"Can't have you getting ahead of yourself."

58

"Me? Couldn't possibly get ahead of myself. Furthest thing from my mind."

She lifted an emerald eye to his, hinting at a smile.

"We'll have to enjoy it until I leave for El Paso."

"El Paso?"

"They released Don Victor. He's set up shop in El Paso. Briscoe is down there keeping an eye on things. I'm to relieve him in a couple of weeks."

"Will you be gone long?"

"Hard to say. Depends on what he's up to."

"He wasn't in prison very long."

"No, he wasn't. Good lawyers and questionable judicial judgment got him off on appeal."

"And so, he will have you running off again."

"You make it sound like it matters. Next thing you know, I just might get ahead of myself."

"Furthest thing from your mind. You said so yourself."

"I'm just saying fair warning."

"What if it does?"

"What if it does what?"

"Matter."

"I'd like that."

"You would?"

"You know I would." He lifted her chin. Her lashes drifted. He swept her up in a kiss meant to be. Ahead of himself, first thing comes to mind.

Topeka

Atkins let Esteban's report sink in and smolder. The Knights of Labor man met with Chorus, why? There could only be one reason. Palmer is trying to raise the money to finance Royal Gorge construction. Chorus knows the value of that right-of-way to his D&RG shares. If a work stoppage delays us, it buys time for Palmer. Pinkerton can break the strike. They can't build a trestle.

"Chorus is paying for the strike," he said.

"It would appear so," Esteban said.

"The best way to stop the strike is to cut off the money." He leveled his gaze at the Spaniard.

"I believe you have friends who can arrange such a thing."

"Sí. It will be expensive."

"Not as expensive as losing that right-of-way. Arrange it."

The Spaniard rose. As expected, the matter in hand.

El Paso

Days passed, a week, then two. Comings and goings at the El Anillo hacienda proved no more interesting than weekly supply trips to El Paso. Then early one afternoon, the ferret-faced Escobar drove a carriage into town. Cane followed. In town, Escobar parked around the corner from the stage office. He lit a cigar and settled in to wait. Something may be up. Likely arriving on the stage.

Cane drew rein up the block and stepped down at a café. He took a window table with a view of the stage office. He ordered pie and coffee. The Santa Fe stage rolled in at three o'clock, thirty minutes late. It disgorged passengers and mail. Among the passengers, a tall dark-skinned man in a dark suit who separated himself from the knot awaiting baggage. He headed straight for Escobar's carriage and climbed in. The carriage rolled out of town.

Cane tossed coins on the table and collected his horse for the ride back to the hacienda.

Escobar led the way down a long lamplit tiled corridor in the gathering evening. They found Patrón in his study.

"Don Victor, it is good to see you free of incarceration," Esteban said.

"It is good to be free of incarceration." The Don extended his hand in greeting.

"Have a seat." He motioned to leather chairs drawn up around a fireplace dominating one end of the room, quiet in warm weather season. "Tequila?"

"Por favor."

"Escobar, tequilas, and one for yourself."

Escobar poured at a sideboard and served from a silver tray. He set the bottle close at hand and took his seat.

The Don lifted his glass. "Salud."

"Salud." Glasses drained and refilled.

"Now, amigo, tell us, what might we do for you?"

"We have a client who wishes a problem eliminated. I obtained the usual fee. Twenty thousand, half now and half on execution."

"And does this problem have a name?"

"Eli Chorus."

"The anarchist financier." Don Victor pursed his lips and fingered his mustache.

"Is there a problem with this?" Esteban asked.

"No. Only the wonder no one has seen the necessity of this before now. Who is this client?"

"Stephen Atkins."

"The railroad man."

"Sí."

"What makes Chorus a problem to him? Not that it matters more than curiosity."

"Chorus is backing the Knights of Labor organizing a union strike against his build out of the Royal Gorge spur."

"Meddlesome old Eli. Sooner or later he was bound to take

steps too far for his own good. Escobar, my son. Can you see to this?"

"Sí, Patrón."

"Bueno!" He lifted his glass. "To problem solved. Salud!"

CHAPTER ELEVEN

Early the following morning the carriage rolled out headed for town. Cane observed the dark stranger and the ferret driven by a peon. The carriage carried luggage, suggesting they were bound for either the depot or stage office. Cane swung into the saddle and picked up a slow lope down the trail.

He gave the Don's men a good start. Once in the low hills he left the main trail, giving the carriage a wide berth, he raced ahead to town. He bet on the stage office, swung down at a rail up the street, and took up his watch in the shadows of a nearby alley. Minutes later the carriage reined to a stop. Escobar and the stranger unloaded their bags and stepped inside to the ticket counter as the peon wheeled away.

Destination was an easy deduction for this leg. The way north led to Santa Fe. The best he could do without detection would be to follow a day delayed. He didn't like that option, but he couldn't think of a better alternative. As luck would have it, the men left the office and took seats on a boardwalk bench to await the stage where they might talk freely. From the alley, Cane was able to overhear snatches of what was said.

"Where will I find this Chorus?" Escobar asked.

"He has a secluded mansion at Manitou Springs, north of Pueblo. I have drawn a map. It is crude but it should lead you there." He passed a folded paper Escobar tucked in his coat pocket.

"Security?"

The rattle of a passing wagon, creaking wheels, and the jangle of harness tack drowned out the reply. More mumbling followed before the northbound stage hauled lines to a halt at the office.

Cane slipped away to the back of the alley and headed for the Western Union office. They'd given him a much better option than a day-delayed pursuit. Chorus, Manitou Springs, but why the question about security?

Great Western Detective League Offices
Denver

"Beau!" Crook waved from his office door.

Longstreet sensed urgency in the summons as he strode across the office.

"What is it?"

The answer offered was another telegram from Cane. The Don's man and an unknown accomplice were headed to Manitou Springs to find someone named Chorus.

"Looks like something is up. Ever heard of Chorus?"

"Eli Chorus. Wealthy financier. Don't know much about him, though rumors occasionally link him to shady investments or civil disturbances. Nothing has ever been proven."

"What do you suppose El Anillo wants with him?"

"Hard to say. Whatever it is, it has them curious about security."

"I'd say they don't expect to be welcomed with open arms."

"Sounds that way. Beau, you need to get there first. Keep an eye on things and see what develops."

O'Rourke House

Longstreet jogged the blue roan he'd dubbed Yankee up to the fence and stepped down. Privately the name amused him. He found a certain humor in a former confederate officer riding a blue-coated horse named Yankee. It made defeat seem somehow less total. He looped a rein over the front fence, swung through the gate to a groan, and dashed up the steps. The door opened to the smell of baking bread. Maddie poked her head out of the kitchen, smiled, then sobered at the prospect of what matter might bring him home this time of day. She crossed the dining room wiping her hands on her apron.

"Sure and I expect you'll be off somewhere now."

"Afraid so."

She followed him up the stairs to his room. She stood in the doorway watching him pack.

"Where to this time?"

"Manitou Springs. Briscoe wired us, Don Victor's boys are headed there."

"Does this mean you don't have to go to El Paso?"

"Don't know. We'll have to see what Manitou Springs brings."

He clasped his saddlebags on a fresh change of clothes and tossed his bedroll on the bed next to it.

"Can I fix you something for the trail?"

"I'll provision up in town."

"It's late to be leaving today. Couldn't you get an early start in the morning?"

He caught her eye.

"If I wasn't afraid of getting ahead of myself, I might think you didn't want me to go."

"I don't."

"Good." He took her in his arms.

She held on tight.

He took in her scents. Fresh bread and vanilla. Minutes passed. He touched her cheek.

She made as if to let him go.

"I don't want to go either."

She smiled dewy-eyed at that.

The moment melted in a kiss neither could deny nor dismiss before life demanded breath.

"You're right. I'll ride into town, provision up, and leave in the morning."

What more could be said?

Nothing for a kiss.

Pueblo

They trooped off the train, a dozen burly men in ill-fitting suits and derby hats. They massed on the platform under bright blue sky and brilliant sunshine. Trevane stepped forward to meet them, introducing himself as lead agent. They stepped aside as she detrained to the platform.

Pinkerton agent Samantha Maples was a disarming dark-eyed beauty with blue-black hair, flawless complexion, and spectacular figure. Trevane smiled broadly. She arched a brow with a knowing half-smile.

"Trevor, so you're running this operation. What a pleasant surprise." She lifted her chin to the guard detachment. "I begin to understand now why I'm paired with this . . . show of force."

Trevane offered his arm. She took it. "This way, gentlemen."

He led his team up the street to the hotel. Inside the deserted lobby he gathered the men.

"Stick close by the hotel. We don't want to attract any attention and I need to know where to find you in the event of trouble. If you go out, do so no more than in pairs. Understood?" Heads nodded and turned to the registration desk.

"Well that takes care of them. What of me?"

"We're a pair."

"Hmmm. Yes, I've heard that before. Is that all there is to this assignment for me?"

"Afraid I'm not that lucky."

"If not luck, then what?"

"You have a subject of interest."

"I do. Now what subject have you got that interests me?"

"Come along. We'll have some supper and I'll show you along the way."

Leaving the hotel, they took a leisurely stroll down the boardwalk toward the west end of town and the end of track worksite. Trevane paused at the batwings to a saloon. Silver Spike, Samantha read the sign. Inside, the union organizer held court at the bar. Trevor lifted his chin.

"He's your person of interest."

"Which him?"

"The one doing all the talking."

"What's our interest in him?"

"That's what supper is for."

"And here I thought we were our interest for supper."

"We are of course but that comes with dessert."

"My faith is restored."

A short stroll back toward the hotel in gathering shadow led to the Colorado Café, a cut-above eatery by Pueblo standards. They were shown to a candlelit table complete with linen, silver, and china. Trevane ordered a bottle of claret and steaks.

"So, what's our interest in him?" Samantha asked.

"He's the Knights of Labor organizer. Our client believes he's been put up to this by person or persons unknown."

"Why do they believe that? The Knights organize unions all the time."

"True, but the timing of this one seems too much to credit to coincidence. The AT&S secures right-of-way to a lucrative silver strike from a reluctant rival and the next thing you know, the Knights are here, stirring up work stoppage trouble."

The waiter arrived with the wine. Trevor sampled it with a nod. The waiter filled their glasses and departed. Trevor lifted his glass.

"To good times past and yet to come."

Samantha smiled. "That sure, are we?" She touched his glass and joined him in a sip.

"Who's the reluctant rival?"

"The Denver & Rio Grande."

"If they're reluctant, why did they give up the right-of-way?"

"They didn't exactly give it up. They leased it under pressure from creditors who were reluctant to finance the Royal Gorge spur."

"Find other investors."

"That takes time. The current investors saw an opportunity to profit from the right-of-way without taking the risk of developing it."

"So the Knights of Labor show up to slow down D&RG's competitor until D&RG can raise the money to take its property back. If there is a sponsor to the 'coincidence,' I'd start there."

"Possibly. Then again, dancing with the devil might invite its own labor troubles. If there is a sponsor footing the bill, we simply don't know who it is."

"And that's where I come in, 'dancing with the devil' as you phrase it."

"Those devastating charms of yours are more than up to the task."

The waiter returned with sizzling steaks and dollops of creamy mashed potatoes. He refilled their glasses and departed again.

"Devastating, I don't know as I've ever been described that way before."

"I'm devastated."

She laughed. "We are sure now, aren't we?"

CHAPTER TWELVE

Pueblo

Longstreet rode into town under bright sunshine. He drew rein at the stage office and stepped down. He made a quick check of the schedule. Next northbound wasn't due until noon. Time to check into the hotel. He swung back into the saddle and jogged up the street.

Muted sun turned the lobby a tawny glow. Polished wood and red velvet offered welcome. He stepped up to the registration desk.

"May I be of service?"

"A room."

"How long will you be staying with us, Mr. . . . ?" He spun the register.

"Longstreet." A familiar scent.

"Beau Longstreet, whatever brings you to Pueblo?"

He recognized the honeyed tone, turning around.

"Samantha, my dear, I might ask the same."

"Westbound train for a starter. Company business after that. Your turn."

"Northbound stage, company business."

"Could it be the same business?"

"I doubt it."

"Good, then we'll not be on opposite sides this time. Will you have time to have a drink or some supper?"

"I'll be leaving as soon as my package arrives. I don't know

69

exactly when that might be."

"One of those sudden departures again. Pity."

"Not necessarily. I'll know when the stage arrives at noon."

"A girl can hope then."

"And you?"

"I have a contact to meet. It shouldn't occupy the evening."

"Shall we say 6:30 here and see what will be?"

She smiled and patted his cheek as Trevane turned the banister at the foot of the stairs.

"Longstreet, what are you doing here?"

"Nice to see you too, Trevor. Company business. Sam and I have already discussed it. Not the same business."

"Good." He held out his arm to Samantha. "We have a contact to plan."

She took the offered arm, catching Longstreet's eye with a wink.

"Good day to you both." Longstreet watched them depart. *Samantha.* They had a history. An interesting history actually. But that history came before Maddie. Trevane had inserted himself into their history, not without some encouragement from Sam to be fair. That was then. This is now. Sam knew it. Circumstances permitting, they'd have a pleasant supper sufficient to annoy Trevor, which was probably the point of her invitation. He smiled.

The noon stage arrived an hour late with no sign of Escobar. Further west along the spur approaching Cañon City and the mouth of the gorge, a girl in tattered skirt and peasant blouse pushed a wheelbarrow laden with a barrel of fresh cool water and ladles along the roadbed. Rails and hammers clanged, rising on shimmers of heat. Dust floated here and swirled there stirred up by work and a gusty hot wind. She paused to dispense cool drinks to appreciative crewmen. The water was welcome.

The girl a refreshing distraction from the drudgery of their labors. Her blue-black waves tied up in a red bandanna. Her beauty shown through dust smudges on her cheek and bare shoulder. She smiled, her dark eyes laughing as she bantered away workmen with remarks more ribald than a word of thanks.

Paddy O'Cairn watched her approach with amused interest.

"Drink?" She flashed a bright smile.

"Whiskey?"

She looked in the barrel and shrugged with a frown. "Just water, I'm afraid." She held out a dipper.

He accepted it and drank thirstily. Water dribbled down his chin. His eyes never left her.

"We could have us a whiskey at the Silver Spike after work."

"We've yet to be properly introduced."

"Beggin' your pardon, miss. Paddy O'Cairn." He doffed his cap with an exaggerated bow.

"Mary Miller," she said in mock curtsy.

"I've not seen you on the line before, Mary Miller."

"I've only just been hired."

"Then you've yet to join the union."

"Union?"

"The Knights of Labor. We're organized here. I serve as steward. If you'll join me for that whiskey, I'll be pleased to sign you in." His eyes smiled something more than amused.

"Ah, if it's business then I suppose I might just this once. The Silver Spike you said."

"The very one."

"Good then. I shall make one my limit."

She pushed on, leaving his eyes to follow her hips.

Silver Spike

Samantha peered over the top of the batwings. The saloon was crowded with railroad construction men fresh off their day's labor. Smoke filled the air along with lively boisterous chatter. O'Cairn sat at a visible table near the bar with a bottle and two glasses. She put on her Mary Miller and pushed into the saloon uncertain. He waved. She smiled. The crowd parted for her passing. Admiring glances followed her to his table.

"Have a seat." He poured and lifted his glass. "Welcome to the Knights of Labor."

She lifted her glass. He tossed off his. She took a sip.

"So, these Knights of Labor accept lady knights?"

"It's not unheard of, though as you might imagine, it is not all that common either."

"I suppose that makes it something of an honor then."

He chuckled. "You might think of it that way if you wish. I should think it a pleasure to have you join us."

"And what must that all entail?"

He drew a card and the stub of a pencil from his jacket pocket. "Sign here."

"And just exactly what is it I get for signing here?"

"We represent you in labor negotiations with the company."

"What negotiations?"

"Wages and working conditions at the moment. We are seeking a ten percent wage increase with a fifty percent premium for aerial work on the trestle, though that last bit likely doesn't interest you."

"What makes you so sure?"

"Hanging in a rope harness to guide and secure timbers into place? Dangerous work that and not suited to the gentle sex."

"Gentle sex is it?" She baited him with a look to take him where he wished. "Still ten percent is better than a poke with a stick." She picked up the pencil and signed.

"That's the girl." He lifted his glass. "To the Knights." He tossed off his drink.

She finished hers.

"Another?"

"One is my limit, today."

"Tomorrow then?"

"We shall see." She favored him with another promising look.

If she hurried, she had just enough time to clean up and meet Longstreet for dinner. Trevor would be salty. Delicious.

CHAPTER THIRTEEN

Samantha swept into the lobby promptly at 6:30 fresh from bathing away any vestiges of Mary Miller. Longstreet smiled.

"The lady is punctual."

"I took a chance you hadn't left town."

"Not yet. Have a good day?"

"Only if you consider pushing a barrel of water around a railroad construction site all day good."

"Working for Pinkerton is as glamorous as ever."

"I'll wager you never pulled duty like that."

"Why on earth would they put you up to an assignment like that?"

"Buy me a drink and some dinner."

He extended his arm.

Across the lobby Trevane scowled.

Samantha took Longstreet's arm, amused at Trevor's displeasure. She guided Longstreet along the boardwalk to the Colorado Café. Settled comfortably at a candlelit table, Longstreet ordered a bottle of sherry.

"I take it you're working for the AT&S," Longstreet said. "Anything special?"

"Not really. Routine labor dispute. What are you up to?"

"Company business, not routine."

"Sounds exciting."

The waiter arrived with their drinks and poured. They ordered the house special, roast chicken with buttered potatoes and wilted greens.

Samantha lifted her glass. "To good times past, Beau Long-street."

"To good times." Glasses touched and sipped.

"So, when we last left you, you and Maddie were trying to sort out your feelings for each other."

"We were, weren't we."

"And?"

"We've made progress."

"Progress. What's that?"

"I'm leaning."

"You're leaning. You're talking in riddles."

"I'm considering . . ."

"You're considering what? Marriage?"

"I'm considering it."

"I guess then that leaves us precisely where we left it the last time. Marriage is a big step, Beau. If it takes too much 'considering' you may not be ready for it. I'll say this, if it was me, you'd damn well better get to it or vacate the privy."

The house special appeared, sparing further discussion for the moment. They finished off the last glasses of sherry over peach cobbler.

"I don't see what's so difficult, Beau. Either you love the woman or you don't."

"I do love her."

"Well, we've got 'love her' in hand. Next comes 'I do.' "

"Easy for you to say."

" 'Tis not. If it were, I'd likely have said so by now. At least I know who I am. In your case, I'm not so sure."

"Not so sure you know?"

"No. Not so sure *you* know."

She had a point. A ring of truth like a gong.

"I suggest you pay some attention to yourself, Beau Longstreet. In all fairness to Maddie. It's been lovely. Thank you for dinner. If you'll excuse me, I see some of my colleagues have arrived." She rose and patted his cheek. "It's for the best."

Trevor rescued Samantha's evening, arriving for supper with one of the Pinkerton guards. She accepted his offer of an after-dinner drink.

"Enjoy yourself?" he asked with an edge.

She smiled. "Old friends. You understand."

Longstreet had a hunch. Counting the days since Cane's wire from El Paso he expected the Don's man to arrive today, or maybe tomorrow if one of the stage legs of the trip had a delay. He'd provisioned up and had Yankee saddled and tethered in the next block up from the station, just in case. He found a shaded porch down the street with a good view of the platform and settled in to wait.

The sun rode high toward the scheduled noon arrival. Longstreet mulled the possibilities. The Don is sending his most trusted operative to Manitou Springs. Why? There's next to nothing there other than the shadow of Pikes Peak at certain times of the day. El Anillo plays for high stakes. What sort of high stake plays out in the middle of nowhere? It didn't make sense. Counterfeit bonds, diamonds, they made sense. Mountain shadows did not. It might yet prove a fool's errand, but they had no choice. They'd have to play it out.

Time crawled past noon. One o'clock became two. Two crept to two-thirty when the northbound wheeled onto Front Street at the west end of town. The lathered team strained in their traces as the driver urged them home before hauling lines at the station. The driver set the brake and climbed down from the box. He opened the coach door, rounding the coach to the luggage boot. Passengers climbed down.

Longstreet kept a keen eye. A tall dark-skinned hombre

stepped down, glancing left and right. Not his man. The next man Longstreet recognized, smaller and ferret-faced. The two collected their bags and departed the station. Longstreet stepped off his porch into the street and made his way to the front of the station in time to observe both men turn north on Main Street toward the hotel. He swung in a block behind them, following on the opposite side of the street.

They paused at the hotel. The tall stranger said something and went inside. Escobar continued on up the street. Longstreet ignored the stranger and followed his man to a seedy bordello in the red-light district. Longstreet remembered the ferret's preference for lodging in such places. He found a shaded bench in front of a barbershop where he took up watch.

Some minutes later Escobar reemerged. He headed back toward the center of town. He stopped at the livery stable where he arranged for a horse. He led the horse down the block and across the street to a general store where he provisioned himself for the trail. With his supplies aboard, he swung into the saddle and rode up the street to the brothel. He put up the horse and supplies before disappearing inside.

Sweet dreams, Longstreet thought. He'll be spending the night. Best be prepared for an early departure. He collected Yankee and stepped into the saddle. He rode out of town on the road north toward Manitou Springs. He found a stream-fed thicket of aspens west of the trail and made camp as the sun slipped behind purple peaks in a fiery display of pink and orange painted in broad strokes against a violet sky.

The moon rose over a diamond studded sky as he sat beside a small fire, sipping coffee after a modest trail supper. His mind drifted to Samantha and her admonition to take care of business or get out of the privy. *Get out of the privy.* She certainly had a way with coming to the nub of the matter. A woman's word was likely sound advice where a woman was concerned.

Maddie was all of that. Rare by his considerable experience, though none of that experience approached the possibilities he saw in Maddie O'Rourke. Possibilities even for a man like him.

A man like him. She'd raised that question too. Who or what was this man like him? He probed his thoughts for some settled down version of himself. Who might that be? He'd come this far on his own. He'd cut his ties with home and war in bitter defeat. He'd drifted west from opportunity to opportunity, making his way in a world of the moment with little thought given to the future, let alone a future shared with someone like Maddie. No not someone *like Maddie*. With Maddie. A settled down future spoke of something more than the moment. What more?

He tossed the last dregs of his coffee, then rolled up in his blanket and rested his head on the soft side of a saddlebag pillow stuffed with spare clothing. He held Maddie in his thoughts. She seemed to watch him expectantly. He reached out to her as in a dream. A dream intruded on by the feeling Samantha stood behind him, looking over his shoulder, tapping her foot impatiently. They had a history. The questions hung in the future.

CHAPTER FOURTEEN

Longstreet woke before dawn. He coaxed the coals of his small fire to heat the remains of last night's coffee. He grained, watered, and saddled Yankee for the trail. He poured a morning cup of coffee to go with a hard tack biscuit. The sky grayed to first light as he finished his breakfast. He kicked dirt over the remains of his fire and settled into the aspens to watch the trail south.

A bright ball of full-up sunlight lanced across the eastern plain to a purple shadowed rider on the trail from the south. Longstreet watched the rider approach, anticipating his man well before he could identify him. Escobar jogged his horse past the thicket where Longstreet might have hit him with a stone. Longstreet let the El Anillo man continue north before stepping into the saddle and wheeling away north on his trail.

One didn't question the Don's means and methods. Don Victor considered Escobar his most trusted operative. Still, with the amount of money at stake in this job, Esteban would leave nothing to chance. He'd departed Pueblo shortly after his arrival, reaching Chorus's hacienda near sunset. He settled into a wooded hillside just east of the hacienda, a vantage point from which he could observe events as they might unfold.

The Don's man left the main trail south of Manitou Springs, following a second trail northwest into the hills. Longstreet

79

tracked along behind, the man's purpose growing more curious by the hour. Toward midday the trail crested onto a shallow shelf of a plateau. Longstreet drew rein in the trees south of the clearing. A stately stone mansion dominated the far side of the clearing backed up by a forested approach to a shear rock wall.

Across the clearing, Escobar stepped down at the gate to a small, fenced yard. He looped a rein at the rail and stalked his way to a broad stone veranda fronting the formal front entrance. Longstreet drew a telescope from his saddlebag, extended the tube, and fitted it to his eye.

Escobar banged a heavy brass knocker and waited. Presently the doors swung open to an ebony giant in a white coat. Longstreet couldn't make out the exchange between the two. Escobar offered the manservant what appeared to be a calling card. The card slipped and fell to the doorframe. The giant bent to fetch it. Escobar struck with the speed of a snake, steel flashed, severing the giant's throat. The assailant stepped aside. The blood-soaked white coat toppled onto the veranda. The assassin entered the house.

Longstreet snapped his glass closed and spurred the blue roan onto the plateau at a gallop to the mansion gate.

Escobar paused, allowing his eyes to adjust to dim light in a dark wood-paneled foyer. Paneled corridors framed a circular center entrance stairway rising to the upper floors. *Where to find him?*

"Who is it, Cyril?"

The thin reedy voice called down from somewhere above. Escobar smiled. A stair squeaked as he climbed.

Longstreet leaped down from the saddle and bounded up the veranda, drawing his pistol as he stepped over the fallen bodyguard. He ducked into a crouch and crossed the threshold, sweeping the foyer and stairway with his gun. Nothing. *Where?* There on the oriental carpet, a bloody footprint. Another on the stair. He slipped off his boots and started up the stairs.

Seated at an elegant desk in a small private study Eli Chorus grimaced at the silence. Unlike Cyril not to respond. Unease crept to the pit of his stomach. He started to rise as a ferret-faced intruder with beady eyes and drawn gun burst into the study.

Chorus's eyes went round in surprise. "What is the meaning of this?"

Escobar laughed. "So rich. So stupid."

"Cyril!"

"Cyril, I'm afraid, will not be coming to your aid. He is somewhat permanently indisposed."

"What have you done with him?"

"He dropped my card before he could announce my visit."

Cold peril gripped Chorus. He took a step back. "What do you want?"

"You, señor. Dead." He cocked the lethal halo to a .41 Colt Thunderer.

Chorus's gaze froze on the muzzle.

The shot exploded in the confined space of the study. Escobar's forehead erupted in a splatter of red gore, gray matter, and bone shards. His pistol fell to the carpet, discharging a harmless second blast where his body fell.

Chorus sank back against his desk, wide eyed at the tall stranger with the smoking gun who'd just saved his life.

"Are you all right, sir?"

Chorus clutched at his chest. "Yes, yes, thanks to you. To whom do I owe my gratitude?"

"Beau Longstreet, sir. Great Western Detective League at

your service. And if I may ask, sir, who are you?"

"Eli, Eli Chorus."

"Do you have any idea why this man wanted to kill you?"

"I've never seen him before in my life. Who is he?"

"Goes by the name Escobar, or did. Works for Don Victor Carnicero. Does that name mean anything to you?"

Chorus squinted, his mind racing. "No, no, can't say that it does."

"The Don heads a network they call El Anillo, the ring. They specialize in high stakes criminal activity, including, it would appear, murder for hire. Do you know anyone who might wish you terminal harm enough to put up big money to have you killed?"

Chorus's mind raced. Provocative question that. One for the moment best left unanswered. "No, I can't think of a soul. I live a quiet life here, secluded, private."

The investigator in Longstreet sensed something less than forthright about the answer. "Well, your circumstance is secluded and private; I'll give you that. As for quiet, we've got a couple of bodies on our hands."

"Alejandro, the cook, has gone to the Springs for supplies this morning. We can see to laying poor Cyril to rest when he returns."

"Then if you'll spare me the use of a blanket, I'll take this one to Denver."

"Anything to be rid of that dreadful creature. Besides my thanks, may I ask how you happened along when you did?"

"We've been keeping an eye on the Don since he got out of prison. We weren't sure what he was up to, only that knowing him, sooner or later it would be something."

"But why murder me?"

"If you don't know the answer to that Mr. Chorus, I'm sure

we don't know either. You may want to give that some thought though. If you have any idea, we may be able to help you."

Esteban watched the big stranger carry what could only be Escobar's blanket-rolled body and tie it across the saddle of his horse. The stranger helped Chorus roll the black giant in a blanket. They bid their farewells. The stranger climbed into the blue roan's saddle with Escobar's horse on a lead. He wheeled away down the trail to the main road.

Esteban feared the worst from the discharge of the second shot. A second attempt would be needed to fulfill the contract on Chorus. The Don would be volcanic at the loss of the man he treated as his son. But first, who is this stranger and why was he following Escobar? He needed the answer to that question before notifying Don Victor of his loss.

He collected his horse, stepped into the saddle, and trailed out after the tall stranger.

CHAPTER FIFTEEN

Denver

Crook lit his desk lamp against the onset of early evening and trimmed the wick. Longstreet lounged in a side chair across the desk, tired at the end of a long day.

"What do you make of it?" Crook asked.

"They're back in business. Murder for hire would be my guess."

"But why him? Why some rich old gentleman living in the hills?"

"Rich old gentlemen have enemies too."

"You said he has no idea who might have wanted him killed, let alone enough to pay an El Anillo price for the work."

"That's what he said."

"Do you believe him?"

"Now there's an interesting question. If we accept the notion rich old gentlemen have enemies too, then there's a good chance he knows who that might be. If he's not telling us what he knows, that begs the question why would he lie? What does Chorus himself have to cover up?"

"What if it's not murder for hire? What if he crossed the Don somehow and this was about payback?"

"That's possible too, but if that's the case, he's covering something up because El Anillo doesn't deal in philanthropic good works. Either way, we don't have much to go on."

"And Escobar isn't talking."

"He's as talkative now as he was the last time we had a collar on him."

"Still, it would have been nice to try to sweat him."

"Couldn't be helped. It was either kill him or he kills the old man."

"You said there was someone with him when he got off the train in Pueblo. What happened to him?"

"They parted company shortly after they arrived. I stayed with my man. You think there's a connection?"

"Can't rule it out. What did he look like?"

"Another Mexican. Big one though, looked like he may have had some Spaniard to him."

"You think he may have stayed in Pueblo?"

"It's possible."

Crook drummed his fingers in thought. "I'll wire Cane to meet you in Pueblo in a few days. No sense leaving him in El Paso. We know where to find the Don when the time comes. The two of you have a look around to see if you can spot the Spaniard."

O'Rourke House
Longstreet swung through the front door to the welcome scents of home.

"It's me."

Maddie poked her head out the kitchen door. "Sure and now look what the cat's dragged in." She smiled and crossed the dining room, wiping her hands to a welcoming kiss. A light step on the stairs parted them suddenly.

"Evening, Mrs. Fitzwalter." Longstreet covered Maddie's embarrassed blush.

"Oh, you two. Don't mind me. I'm old, I'm not dead."

"Cat's out of the bag," Maddie said.

"What cat? It's been all over both of your faces for ever so long. So let's not bother with the charade any longer, shall we?"

"I , . . . we didn't mean anything by it," Maddie said.

"Of course you did. Now give the man a proper welcome home while I go stir whatever might burn in the kitchen."

Longstreet smiled. "I feel better."

"I'm embarrassed."

"Of me?"

"No, silly. Of me."

"Why ever for?"

"The respectability of the house."

He glanced around. "House doesn't seem to be falling down."

"It is still standing, isn't it. Imagine that."

"I have."

Lounging in the shadow of a gnarled old oak across the street, Esteban watched the silhouettes in the window glass. *A woman.* He filed the shadowy display of affection away with the pattern building around the big detective.

El Paso

The Don hated telegrams. They seldom bore good news and whatever the message it was exposed to too many eyes. He tore the envelope open and read.

Death in the family. Survived by intended.

Esteban, the realization dawned like a hot knife plunged into his gut. Black rage rose in a gorge of hot bile, boiling to a fever of vengeance. How? Why? Who? Yes, who. *There will be blood, my son. Your death shall not go unavenged. There will be blood.*

"Julio, wire Esteban to meet me in Pueblo. We depart in the morning."

The giant peon nodded and left to do his master's bidding.

Topeka

Atkins furrowed his eyes into slits. He read the telegram again.

We experienced a delay in filling your order.

A delay. At these prices? Preventing delay was the whole point of his so called "order." Now what? Esteban's friends could be counted upon to finish the job, but delay. What might that mean?

He clasped his hands behind his back. What more could be done? Pinkerton.

O'Rourke House
1910

I scribbled the last of my notes before the thoughts left me. Cane watched. At last I put my pencil to rest.

"Well, I expect that stirred up something of a firestorm."

"It did. The Don didn't take kindly to news of Escobar's death."

"I'm not sure I understand Esteban's role in all this."

"We didn't either at the time. Be patient. That's what makes it a story."

"Patient. You're as bad as the Colonel was in such matters. 'Don't go getting ahead of yourself, Robert,' he'd say."

"Sound advice where investigation is concerned."

"But I'm not investigating. I'm writing a story."

"A story that will be better if you write it like it is an investigation, because it was."

I furrowed my brow at his logic, grudging to conclude he was probably right.

"Will you be staying for lunch, Robert?"

I hadn't noticed Angela appear in the parlor entry. "No, no, thank you, ma'am. A very kind offer, but Penny and I are attending a matinee moving picture show."

She smiled. "How are the wedding plans progressing?"

She had me there. I did as I was told, and at the moment

nothing seemed required, though I had no sense of what might possibly remain to be done. "Everything seems to be progressing satisfactorily." It didn't sound convincing even to me, but it was all I could think of.

"Have you selected a cake yet?"

"Cake? Ah, I don't believe so."

"Mrs. Armitage of my Ladies' Aid Society owns a fine bakery over on Fourteenth Street. She does a very fine cake. You should consider it."

"Sounds like excellent advice. I shall mention it to Penny this very afternoon."

"Splendid. Well then, Briscoe, it appears it will be just you and me for lunch."

She said it with a twinkle in her eye and the barest flush to her cheek.

Cane gave me a conspiratorial wink. "It does then, doesn't it, Angela. I can only hope my company doesn't bore you to death."

"Nonsense." She said it with a girlish laugh. "Good day to you, Robert."

"Good day to you too, ma'am." She was off to the kitchen in a flourish of skirt. Cane watched her go. I wondered.

" 'Til next week then, Robert?"

" 'Til next week." I closed my notebook and took my leave.

Cane listened to the soft, domestic sounds of lunch preparations coming from the kitchen. *Angela.* He smiled. Young Robert might be on to something with this nuptial business. Too bad he hadn't entertained such thoughts in his younger years. There hadn't been an Angela in his younger years. True enough. Then he hadn't slowed down long enough to notice one if he'd bumped into her on the street. Too much water under that bridge now.

"Briscoe."

He unpacked himself from his chair and followed her summons to the kitchen door. He found her hands on hips, glaring at a Mason jar of canned tomatoes.

"Trouble?"

She nodded. "The usual."

He picked up the jar and gave the stubborn lid a twist. It held firm. "I say, you sealed this one for keeps."

"It would appear so."

He gave it a good go. The seal gave off a whoosh.

"That's better." He handed her the open jar. "I guess that renders me of some use."

"Just often enough to justify your keep." A mischievous glint lit her eye.

"I'm relieved to hear that. From time to time I do worry."

"You? Worry? I seriously doubt that."

"Don't. It's true. It passes though."

"Of that I'm quite sure."

"It's the thought of how devastated you'd be without me."

"Devastated." She laughed.

"You would."

"I'm quite sure I could suffer my way through a jar of tomatoes."

"Not that. This." He swept her up in a kiss made to be meant.

She fought, determined for but a moment before giving herself up to the moment.

"See?"

"You're incorrigible."

"Not sure what that means. I do like to help you with a stubborn jar now and then."

"Is that all?"

"Not exactly."

"I didn't think so. Me either." She hugged him.

"What's for lunch?"

★ ★ ★ ★ ★

The motion picture was a western starring Mr. William S. Hart. The story was quite exciting. With the heroine in peril, our hero faced and overcame all manner of harrowing circumstances and villainous deeds to come to her aid. In one scene he raced a train on horseback, leaping from his magnificent animal at full gallop onto the train. He climbed to the top of the mail car to confront a would-be train robber. A fistfight ensued atop the moving train. My Penny covered her eyes and I must admit my heart was in my throat at the raw danger we witnessed. The actual end of the fight was never seen as the train entered a black tunnel, only to emerge on the other side with only our hero standing. The train robbery foiled, our hero next cornered the outlaw gang in its hideout. Facing seemingly insurmountable odds, Mr. Hart managed to prevail in a gun battle with the gang in time to rescue our heroine from a charlatan bent on cheating her of her father's ranch. With order restored hero and heroine ride off into the sunset. We left the theater breathless from the breakneck pace of excitement. Our usual ice cream sundaes seemed the prudent way to restore serenity to our Saturday afternoon.

We settled in to our favorite parlor, Penny with her butterscotch and me, my fudge.

"What do you think, Robert, yellow cake or devil's food?"

"What do I think? I think I like them both in their place."

"I'm sure, but which for our wedding cake?"

"Oh, I hadn't thought of that."

"Well, do. We must make a choice."

I thought over a spoonful of vanilla and fudge. "Devil's food sounds a bit dire for the occasion of a wedding."

"Most people like chocolate. Look at you."

"Yes, I suppose that's true enough. Very well then, devil's food it is."

"On the other hand, yellow cake is more neutral, don't you think? More like a flavor everyone can appreciate."

"If you say so, my dear. Funny you should bring up cake. Only this morning Angela inquired as to if we had made a selection."

"Did she? Did she express preference for a flavor?"

"No, but she did recommend a baker. A member of her Ladies' Aid Society, a Mrs. Armitage, if I'm not mistaken, maintains a bakery on Fourteenth Street, I believe. Do you know it?"

"I do. Very nice, but a little on the pricey side."

"Well, she comes highly recommended. I expect she could even help with that troublesome choice of a flavor."

"I suppose she could, but then comes the price."

I patted her hand. "Don't trouble yourself over that. I've had good news from my publisher this week. The new book is doing quite well and it seems to have revived interest in the first."

Her brows lifted in a lovely look of surprise. "Oh, Robert. That's wonderful news."

"It is." We raised our spoons in mock toast. A spoon of her caramel for me, a bit of my fudge for her. "Splendid. It's settled then."

"Settled? We still don't know what flavor."

CHAPTER SIXTEEN

Silver Spike
Pueblo

She parted the batwings to peek inside, as though too timid to enter. O'Cairn, holding court at the end of the bar, seemed to sense her presence like a moth to a candle flame. He broke away from his admirers, threading his way through the crowded saloon. He smiled a welcome mixed of pleasure and something more male. Perfect.

"Mary, isn't it?"

" 'Tis."

"What brings you by?"

"I've only been thinking and it's given me a question."

"Anything I can help with?"

"I suppose. It's about the union."

"If you permit me to buy you a drink, I shall attempt to answer it for you."

She bit her lip, as though uncertain. Innocent. "I suppose."

"Come this way." He held the batwing for her.

He took her by the arm and led the way to a back corner table that might pass for as quiet as could be expected on the fringe of a raucous din. Eyes followed her across the room, hungry among the men, predatory among the working girls. He roused a sleepy drunk slumped in one chair and invited him to be a good fellow and find some other accommodation for the lady's sake. He signaled the bartender for a bottle and two glasses. The union organizer struck a dark and handsome figure in a rough-cut way. Attractive really, all circumstances considered. The bottle and glasses arrived. He poured.

"Now there," he lifted his glass. "Tell me about this question that so bedevils a lass as to insist she risk this den of iniquity to gain her answer."

Silver tongued besides. This may prove easier than expected. " 'Tis the strike."

"What about the strike?"

"They can be . . . you know . . . violent."

He shrugged. "I'll nay say it doesn't happen, but we shan't be beggin' it."

"To be sure. 'Tis only that it frightens me."

His gaze softened. "There, there, lass. Have no fear. I'll see you safely far removed from the line should any trouble arise."

"You will?"

"I will. You have my word on it as a gentleman."

"When do you think it might begin?"

"We've given the railroad a month to meet our demands. Another couple weeks to that."

"And do you think they will?"

He smiled mirthlessly. "I rather doubt it."

"So there will be a strike."

"Quite likely."

"What will the railroad do?"

"The railroad? They'll do like industrialist robber barons do. They'll endeavor to break our will. Starvation if they can. Pinkerton if they can't."

"Pinkerton?"

"Private cops. Thugs really. That's where the violence often starts."

"Are all Pinkerton agents thugs?"

"My experience, but don't you worry that pretty head of

yours. You'll be well taken care of."

"I feel so much better."

"Good then. Let's top off that drink, shall we?"

"Mr. O'Cairn, you become temptation to a girl."

"Dare I hope?"

She allowed a glimmer to escape her eye, lifted her glass, and tossed it off.

"Stuffy in here, don't you think?" he said.

"I think it may be the whiskey."

"Come along. We shall see." He picked up the bottle, glasses in hand, and led the way through the crowd to the batwings. The evening air tasted clean and cool. A blanket of stars glittered across the night sky, with a crescent moon on the wane.

"Do you mean to drink in the street?" She giggled the suggestion of inebriation.

"This way."

"This way where?"

"You'll see if you're game."

"Game?"

He led the way down the boardwalk to the ally and a shadowed stairway. He climbed to the top landing and took a seat.

She followed. He poured her a glass as she sat beside him.

"Better?"

" 'Tis." She glanced around. "Where might this lead?"

He tossed off his drink and took her chin on the tip of a finger. "Let see, shall we?"

Paddy O'Cairn, interesting. Company sacrifice no less.

Early morning light suffused the lobby a red-golden hue. A disheveled Samantha Maples crossed carpet and hardwood to the staircase as Trevor descended to the start of his day.

"Up early, or out late?" The casual question, rested on an edge.

"Working."

"I see. Above and beyond?"

"Worth the trouble."

"Trouble? I'm sure."

"Don't be an ass. You wanted to know why the labor trouble now. Better yet, who might be behind it."

"You got all that?"

"Drunk union organizers are talkative."

"Tell me about it."

"After I clean up."

"Are we headed for a strike?"

"It would appear so. End of the month."

"All right, I'll see you when I get back from the mercantile."

"Run out of pomade?"

"Axe handles. Meet me in the dining room for breakfast."

Refreshed and returned to her Victorian persona, Samantha found Trevor in a quiet corner of the dining room, nursing a cup of coffee. He signaled the waiter as she crossed the sunlit room.

"Coffee?"

"Please. Eggs, ham, and a biscuit."

"Make it two," Trevane said.

The waiter scurried off with their order.

"So, what have you got?"

Right to bruised business. She suppressed a smile. "Why now? To slow development of the Royal Gorge spur. Bought and paid for by one Eli Chorus."

"Who the hell is that?"

"Someone with enough money to buy off the Knights."

"Why, what's his angle?"

"You're asking for more than the union organizer knows."

"He has to have a stake in this somewhere. A man doesn't finance labor strife for amusement."

"Who stands to gain if AT&S is delayed?"

"Good question. Where do we find this Eli Chorus?"

"Manitou Springs. Do you plan to question him?"

"We'll see how Strong wants to proceed. You've *managed* to learn what we were asked to find out."

"Did that last little bit stick in your throat?"

"I don't know what you're talking about."

The waiter arrived with their breakfasts.

"Jealousy, Trevor, dear, jealousy."

"Should I be?"

"Every chance you get. It pleases me. Now eat your eggs before they get cold."

"Anything to please."

"I thought as much."

CHAPTER SEVENTEEN

Pinkerton Office
Denver

Well, this is embarrassing. Kingsley lifted his teacup and blew across the steam. *The client informs the head office that force will be needed to disburse strikers who have yet to walk out on strike. It would appear we know management's negotiation posture.* He puzzled at the yellow foolscap lying on his otherwise immaculate desk. *Still, it begs the question: why does head office hear it from the client before I hear from my people on the ground? First things first. Inform Chicago the necessary manpower is in place. Secondly, it seems I'm due to personally look in on the situation in Pueblo.*

Pueblo

Cane and Longstreet canvassed the town in search of some sign of the Spaniard to no avail, if indeed the man were a Spaniard. With no name to work with and only the sparest of descriptions the task came off more hopeful than promising. Prowling the construction site beyond the west end of town in the dusty heat of midday, Cane stopped abruptly.

"What is it?" Longstreet asked.

"Look there." Cane lifted his chin. "The water girl. If that isn't our Pinkerton friend Miss Maples, it should be."

Longstreet chuckled. "It is Sam. Our friend Trevor is in town too."

"What are they doing here?"

"Company business she says. By the look of it, I'd say the company is AT&S. If rumor is to be accorded any credence, the business may have something to do with labor unrest in the offing."

"Labor unrest?"

"The Knights of Labor are said to have organized a union. They put forward demands for a new wage scale, given the risks of trestle track construction. Their demands are unlikely to be welcome in Topeka. Unmet demands lead to strikes. Pinkerton has developed something of a specialty in, shall we say, managing situations like that."

"One part of full service to their industrialist clients. Still, strike breaking hardly seems like an assignment for her."

"Good point. They must have her looking for something undercover."

"You should know."

"Now, now, I'm holding fast to my Maddie."

Cane made a show of popping the lid to his pocket watch. "I'm impressed." He snapped the lid closed. "You're practically monogamous."

"And I shall count on your witness to my defense should the subject come up."

"If need be. Let's think about this though. Labor unrest is likely to delay the Royal Gorge spur at considerable expense to AT&S."

"High stakes."

"High enough to engage El Anillo?"

"Perhaps. But Chorus? Why him?"

"I don't know. Something doesn't smell right. In your current state of monogamy do you still talk to Miss Maples?"

"I do."

"Why don't you see what you can find out? Without compromising your virtue of course."

"Of course."

O'Cairn climbed the steps to the caboose serving as the AT&S field office. Strong sat at his desk bathed in a tawny glow of late afternoon sun.

"What do you want?"

" 'Tis thirty days since we presented our demands. Will they be met?"

"Will they be met, he says. Of course not. This railroad will not be held hostage to the arbitrary demands of some rabble-rousing union organizer."

"That is indeed most unfortunate. The rabble to which you refer are your workers. Your rabble-rouser, as you so colorfully choose to label him, is their duly elected union representation. Your refusal to bargain in good faith, leaves us but one choice."

"And what would that be?"

"Why, shut you down, of course."

"You mean declare an illegal strike."

"Nothing illegal about it. A work stoppage intended to bring management to the bargaining table."

"Bargaining table my ass."

"Suit yourself, Mr. Strong. Either you want the Royal Gorge spur built, or you don't. Either you bargain, or your spur won't be built."

"Get the hell out of my office."

"Most unfortunate, Mr. Strong. You seem in the habit of shortsighted decision making."

"Don't threaten me, O'Cairn."

"I wouldn't dream of it. And that's a promise."

Starlight sparkled on the surface of the whiskey. O'Cairn seemed not to notice, preoccupied in his thoughts.

"You seem distant tonight, Paddy. A girl might think she's lost her charm," Samantha said in her Mary persona.

"Sorry. It's only that bastard Strong. Why can these people not see reason?"

"Money."

"There is that."

"Isn't the intent to delay the Royal Gorge spur?"

"His intent. Mine's always the worker first."

"I thought you were being paid to delay the spur."

"Money again." He tossed off his drink.

"What will you do?"

"Rally the men on the morrow. Walk the following morning. Promise me now."

"Promise what?"

"I'll not see you anywhere near the picket line."

"Why not?"

"Pinkerton."

"You expect trouble?"

"I can feel it."

CHAPTER EIGHTEEN

Trevane awoke to a rap at the door. He rolled out of bed, lit the bedside lamp, and glanced at his watch on the nightstand. Midnight. What the hell was this? The rap sounded again. He grabbed his pistol from its shoulder rig hung on the side chair. Another knock.

"I'm coming." He shuffled to the door. "Who is it?"

"Samantha."

He smiled and opened the door.

"To what do I owe . . ."

She barged into the room still dressed as the water girl. "You can put that away." She tossed her head at his gun.

He holstered the gun. "Spent the evening with your favorite union organizer, I see."

"And good I did. The strike is on for day after tomorrow. You'd best alert Strong and have your men ready."

"We knew it would come to this."

"And it has." She turned to go.

"Must you?"

"Must I what?"

"Run off so soon."

"Trevor, Trevor, Trevor, even at a time like this?"

"No time like the present, even at a time like this."

"At least you're predictable."

101

"Is that all?" He drew her to him.

"Well, there is that too."

The stagecoach driver hauled lines to swirling clouds of hot windblown dust. He set the break and climbed down. Kingsley unfolded himself from the uncomfortable horsehair padded seat and stepped down from the coach. The only passenger, he collected his bag and set off up the boardwalk to the hotel. He inquired after Trevane at registration and dashed off a note to meet in the lobby. He deposited his bag in his room and returned to the lobby where he found Trevane and Agent Maples awaiting him. *Interesting.*

"Trevor, Samantha, pleasure to see you again."

"You as well, Mr. Kingsley." Samantha smiled.

"Please, Reggie to you. Let's have a bite of lunch and you can update me on the situation."

"There's plenty to tell," Trevane said. "If you hadn't just arrived, you'd have found a telegram on your desk."

"Sounds ominous."

"It is."

"Lead the way." Kingsley offered Samantha his arm as Trevor led them to the dining room. Blue plates were ordered all around. Trevane described the imminence of a strike and the disposition of his men. Samantha finished, describing the Chorus connection.

"Have we communicated all this to the client?"

"Not the latest. That only came to us late last night."

Kingsley folded his napkin. "Very well then. Samantha, dear, I suggest you resume your duties as water girl. You are our best eye on the situation as it develops."

"The girl gets all the glamour assignments," she said.

"Trevor, you and I shall report all this to Mr. Strong. We'll need his direction as to how and when to deploy our people. Check, please."

Dust boiled around the end of track construction site driven by a brisk west wind. An AT&S end of track caboose parked with a full view of the construction site with Cañon City and the mouth of the gorge a dark smudge in the distance. W. B. Strong pored over engineering plans for the trestle. Foot scrapes on the car platform caught him up to the door. The Pinkerton Trevane and a gray-bearded gentleman in a bowler hat stepped in.

"Mr. Strong."

"Trevane."

"May I present my superior, managing director of the Denver office, Reginald Kingsley?"

"Mr. Kingsley, W. B. Strong, general manager. Pleased to make your acquaintance. I can only assume this isn't a social call; what can I do for you?"

"We've news of the strike," Trevane said.

"I see. Have a seat."

"The plan is afoot to walk out tomorrow."

"No surprise there. It was only a matter of when. O'Cairn, it seems, isn't one to waste time."

"We'll need your direction on how to proceed. Where and when do you wish us to deploy our men?" Trevane said.

"Do we know how many men will support the strike?"

"Hard to say until the moment of truth."

"I think it best you hold your men in reserve until we see how many cross the picket line. If they are allowed to do so peacefully, we may yet continue our progress. Possibly even recruit Chinese to fill out our ranks. Have your men stand ready should the strikers become . . . unruly."

"We understand," Kingsley said. "I believe you also wished to know who might be behind the organizing effort."

"We did wonder at the timing."

"We've put one of our top agents, Samantha Maples, to that question."

"A woman?"

"A very resourceful operative. She's managed to insinuate herself into O'Cairn's confidence."

"She has? How?"

"By working with your crews."

"I should think I'd have noticed a woman on the crew."

"The water girl."

"She's one of yours?"

"Indeed."

"Remarkable. And what might she have learned?"

"Funding to stimulate your current predicament is being provided by a socially progressive financier by the name of Eli Chorus. Mr. Chorus favors reforms to the social order by such means as may be necessary. Anarchy being a means justified by the end."

"I've heard of him. I'm surprised he'd spend his resources on us."

"Don't be. Our head office in Chicago did a bit of additional digging. It turns out Mr. Chorus holds a rather substantial position in the Denver & Rio Grande."

"That explains it. Palmer is in court as we speak trying to have our lease on the Royal Gorge right-of-way set aside on a technicality. Mr. Atkins will be pleased to hear that. Your people have done a fine bit of investigation, Mr. Kingsley."

"Thank you, sir. Your favorable report to our head office would be most appreciated."

"I'm sure that can be arranged, once we've dealt with our strike."

"Yes, as to that. If you like, I shall join you here in the morning so as to be close to the situation and await your direction."

"Yes, that would be most agreeable."

"Trevor will have command of our men in a warehouse at the west end of town. Should they be needed, you have only to give me the order."

"Very well. You've done this before I take it."

"Personally, no, but the Eye That Never Sleeps prepares us for any contingency. It's the Pinkerton way."

CHAPTER NINETEEN

Samantha wheeled her water barrel down the roadbed past the depot as the noon stage wheeled around the west end of town bound for the station. She paused to wipe her brow with a red bandanna, taking note of a carriage waiting across from the stage office, the sole occupant a tall dark handsome gentleman dressed in a tailored short coat and sombrero. He might have gone for no more notice than that had it not been for the two passengers who made their way across the platform. A hulking goon carried bags for a familiar silver-haired hombre of distinguished bearing. *Don Victor Carnicero, what's he doing here?* Last she knew, he was in Yuma Prison. Clearly he was not. What brought him to Pueblo? It wasn't the scenery.

The Don climbed into the carriage passenger seat beside the driver. They exchanged greetings while the goon stowed their baggage and mounted the rear seat. The driver clucked to the team. The carriage rolled northwest out of town. Samantha watched them go. She had a strong hunch this might have something to do with Longstreet's "company business." She hefted her water barrel and wheeled it down the roadbed to the construction site.

Longstreet jogged the blue roan along the tracks west of town. Sounds of picks, hammers, and rails clanged a rhythmic serenade to extend end of track. Samantha tended her water barrel in the shade of a copse of aspens just north of the tracks.

Longstreet nudged Yankee over to her and stepped down.

"What are you doing here?" she said.

"Happy to see you too."

"I'm working. You'll give me away."

"Your secret is safe with me. May I have a drink of water?"

She ladled a dipper in the bucket. "You didn't ride out here for a drink of water. What's on your mind?"

Longstreet took a swallow. "I'm wondering if there might be a connection between your company business and my company business."

"Funny, I had the same thought earlier today."

"Oh? Why?"

"You first."

"Well, if rumor is to be believed, you, Trevor, and his pals are likely here to deal with the Knights of Labor union trouble. That could spell high stakes trouble for your client. Stakes high enough to justify someone paying up for an El Anillo assassin."

"I knew it."

"Knew what?"

"There is an El Anillo connection. You just missed it. Don Victor and a couple of his men are here. Who did they kill?"

"They didn't. I followed Escobar to his target. You remember the ferret?"

"Hard to forget the slimy little monster."

"No need to trouble yourself about him any longer. I got there in time. Escobar is dead. The intended victim is not."

"Who is it?"

"A reclusive financier, Eli Chorus."

Samantha's eyes went round.

"Something the matter?" Longstreet asked.

"Chorus's money is behind the Knights of Labor."

"Why would he do that?"

"Reggie found out he holds a large position in the Denver &

Rio Grande."

"What do they have to do with this?"

"They own the right-of-way to the Royal Gorge. They've only leased it to the AT&S because they couldn't afford to develop it. They must have gotten their financial house in order. They are suing to have the lease set aside."

"That makes a construction delay their friend. You said Don Victor is here with two of his goons. Could one of them possibly be a big Spaniard?"

"Tall, dark, good-looking, the driver. Possibly. Why?"

"He came up from El Paso with Escobar. They parted company. I stuck with the ferret. We've been looking for him. It's the only lead we had until now."

"So what brings the Don out in the open? Last I knew he was in Yuma."

"Got out on appeal a couple of months ago. Set himself up in a hacienda outside El Paso."

"Another fortress?"

"Something like that. Your question is a good one though. 'What brings him out in the open?' He treated Escobar like a son. Could be that. It could also be unfinished business."

"Chorus."

"Exactly. That still leaves us with another big question."

"What's that?"

"Who put El Anillo up to eliminating Chorus." Longstreet collected Yankee's leads.

"Where are you going?"

"Manitou Springs. That's where they're headed." He toed a stirrup.

"Beau."

He paused.

"Be careful."

He smiled. "Why if I didn't know better . . ."

"Old times' sake. Just be careful."

He swung into the saddle and wheeled away back to town.

Esteban drove a brisk pace up the road to Manitou Springs under bright blue sky dotted in puffball clouds. A tranquil pleasant day belied Don Victor's grim mood.

"Tell me how did it happen? How did my son die?"

"I only observed from the nearby hills. I did not see what happened inside the hacienda. Escobar gained entrance by killing Chorus's giant bodyguard. He must have been followed. No sooner had he entered the house, a lone rider galloped onto the mesa and entered the hacienda behind him. Two shots followed soon after. It gave me a bad feeling. I only knew the outcome when the big stranger came out carrying a body rolled in a blanket. He loaded the body on Escobar's horse and bid an unhurt Chorus goodbye."

"Who is this stranger?"

"I followed him to Denver. He delivered the body to an undertaker. Then went to the sheriff's office. From there he went to the offices of something called the Great Western Detective League."

"Them again."

"You know them?"

"They put me in Yuma. The big man, do you know his name?"

"I visited the undertaker to make sure . . . your son was properly cared for. The undertaker called him Longstreet."

"The very one. That makes two scores to settle with him. He is in Denver, you say."

"Sí, he lives with a woman."

The Don squinted off in thought. "This Chorus's hacienda, it is hidden?"

"It is."

"Bueno. We shall finish our client's contract. We can then

invite this Longstreet to find his way to a slow and painful death. There will be blood, my son. There will be blood shed for your blood."

CHAPTER TWENTY

Topeka

Atkins paced his lamplit office pitched in evening gloom. Strong's wire naming Chorus as the source of his impending labor problems only confirmed what he already knew. Coming on top of the "delay in filling your order" had him vexed. What was wrong? Why hadn't Esteban's friends finished the job? With the strike imminent, what was to be done? Strong would have to judge and deal with the situation on the ground. All he could do was see to it, if he could, that his attorneys prevailed against Palmer's suit to set aside the right-of-way lease. *Damn.*

Pueblo

They packed the smoke-filled Silver Spike, rough men, smudged with the residue of the day's toils. Beer, sweat, and tobacco scented the air in a lamplit yellowish fog. O'Cairn climbed up on the bar to be seen and heard. He wandered the room with his gaze, and caught Samantha's eye in a front corner with half a smile.

"Men!" He raised his hands for silence. "Men!" The buzz settled.

"The time has come. AT&S has rejected our demands."

A rumble of disapproval and anger rolled over the assembly. O'Cairn let the tide of opinion crest and ebb.

"On the morrow we have but one choice. One choice to make our voices heard. One choice to make our voices heard in terms the stone-deaf AT&S must understand. They must understand we will not work under these conditions for these wages. For too long they have abused us. For too long they have ignored our rightful cries. Now we will be heard. Their damn bridge will not be built until they hear us. On the morrow, I will stand for your voice. I will stand for your one chance. I will strike. Are you with me?"

A roar erupted in the room. Aye and aye peppered the din. Fists pumped the air. Beer spilled and quaffed. O'Cairn gave them their moment, gave them their anger. It drew them to him in one mind. The mind of a mob. That was his weapon. He needed it sown, seated, and rooted. Gradually the crowd came back to him, ready to be led.

"In the morning, those who are with me will not report for work. We will form at end of track, barring the next timber or rail to be laid. We will stand firm and resolute until our demands have been met. We will have signs for you there. Everyone must know the right of our grievance and the full measure of our intent. Each sign shall be affixed to a stout handle, should anyone attempt to cross our line forcibly. Am I understood?"

"Aye!" They took up the cry. "Aye" filled the room.

"Then we stand together. Together we stand as one. Together we prevail as one. Are you with me?"

The room exploded in a new round of frenzy. *Sown and rooted. 'Tis done.*

"On the morrow then!" He pumped his fist in the air to yet another roar. He jumped down from the bar into the back-slapping adulation of his mob. They swept him up to the bar rail for courage. All the more on the morrow.

Burly grim-faced men gathered a knot around the glow of a single lamp. The halo disappeared in predawn gloom inside the trackside warehouse stacked in crates and bales smelling of raw wood and hemp. Trevane held court with Kingsley at his elbow.

"According to reports from the rally last night, the strike will commence at dawn. Pickets will be thrown up at end of track. We are to remain on standby here. Mr. Kingsley will be stationed with Mr. Strong in the caboose office. Strong wants to see if any of his crew attempt to cross the picket line. The strikers will carry signs, the handles to which might also serve as clubs. Should any confrontation turn violent we will be called in to disburse the strikers. Your axe handles are stacked there in the corner."

"What if no one crosses?" one of the men asked.

"That becomes Mr. Strong's prerogative," Kingsley said.

"Any questions?" Trevane glanced round the circle.

"Very well then," Kingsley said. "Make yourselves as comfortable as the . . . amenities permit. I shall repair to Strong's office to await developments."

Dawn. They emerged from behind the Silver Spike a long line, signs shouldered, draped in purple shadow. They walked in file behind O'Cairn paralleling the roadbed to end of track. They crossed the roadbed and took up positions between the completed track and the roadbed to Cañon City and the gorge. O'Cairn passed down the line, encouraging each man while making a mental tally of those who stood with him and any that might stand with the company and attempt to cross their line.

Sun shards sliced down the tracks from the east, framing the caboose office in silhouette. Morning light crept toward end of track lifting a curtain of darkness from the arrayed pickets. Strong fitted a telescope to his eye counting their number against the chance of opposition. He offered the glass to Kingsley, who in turn scanned the line. It looked as though the strike was well supported. He passed the glass back. Strong snapped the glass closed.

"He's got most of them. I don't see much chance of significant numbers crossing the line."

"What would you have my men do?"

"For now we watch. We let them sweat the heat of the day. I'll wire Mr. Atkins. I suspect he will have another crew willing to come in and cross the line."

The sun climbed past midday. Samantha pushed her water barrel down the line, offering a cool drink and a smile with ears pricked to the mood of the men and any suggestion of useful information. She reached O'Cairn, who greeted her with concern.

"You don't listen very well, do you?"

"I don't know what you're talking about." She filled a cool dipper.

"I told you I didn't want you anywhere near this line."

"And have you all go thirsty in this heat."

" 'Tis not safe, Mary."

She glanced around. "Seems safe enough, present company excepted."

"Sure and I'm the least of your worries . . . my worries."

"Why, Paddy, what a sweet thing to say. I do believe if I listen to that silver tongue of yours much longer, I shall go deaf to the truth."

" 'Tis truth I speak when it comes to your well-being."

"Now have a care or you'll have me believing your blarney."

"No blarney, lass. 'Tis not safe. There's Pinkerton agents afoot and likely a trainload of strikebreakers headed our way. Now water the boys and get on back to safety."

"Spoken like a man with a claim on my whereabouts."

"I'd fancy that."

She wrinkled her nose with a smile and pushed her cart away.

Men. Such simple creatures. Taking advantage of them is almost unfair.

CHAPTER TWENTY-ONE

Manitou Springs

The secluded stone mansion might have suited Don Victor's taste for quartering El Anillo. But the Don was unimpressed, more occupied with matters at hand. The gardener, pressed into domestic service until a suitable replacement for Cyril could be found, answered the door.

"Señor Chorus," Esteban said.

"He is expecting you?"

"Sí."

"Who may I say is calling?"

Esteban offered his card.

"I am sorry, señor, I do not read."

"Tell him Escobar's brother is here."

The gardener turned to go. Julio stepped past Esteban, clapped a hand over the gardener's mouth, and snapped his neck. He dragged the body out to the plaza. Esteban led the way inside.

"Who is it, Roberto?"

Esteban glanced to the right. The voice came from somewhere beyond a large formal parlor. He signaled Julio to mind the door. He led Don Victor through the polished pegged parlor. The room adjoined an equally spacious dining room. They found Eli Chorus seated at the far end of a long formal dining table eating his lunch. His eyes shot wide at the presence of swarthy Latin strangers reminiscent of his would-be assassin.

"Who are you? What is the meaning of this?"

Don Victor drew his gun. "We are here about my son."

"I don't know what you are talking about."

"My son was shot in this very house."

"The one who came to kill me."

"Sí."

"Why would you kill me? I don't even know you."

"It is business." He cocked his pistol, rolling a bullet into firing position.

"Business. How much are you being paid?"

"My client confidences are not open to discussion."

"I'll double it. Whatever Atkins is paying you. I will pay you twice the amount to kill him. When he is dead your client confidence will be undisturbed."

"How do you know who my client is?"

"You think me dull-witted? Atkins is the one whose wits are addled. Now, will you do it?"

"Business is business." The Don released the cocked hammer and lowered his gun. "Twenty-five thousand now. Twenty-five thousand when the job is done. I shall further require the use of this house for a short time."

Chorus stood.

"Where do you think you are going?"

"To draw a draft for your first payment."

Topeka

Atkins read the wire.

Strike on. Need crew.

Strong

Need crew. Need strikebreakers is more like it. They don't come cheap. Then again, neither do strikes. Atkins drummed his fingers on the desk, gazing out a rain-spattered office window. He'd need men willing to take on rough work. Quite a few for that matter. Where to find them? Who might recruit them? Who could he trust?

Denver

The carriage clopped up the quiet tree-lined street settling into purple onset of evening.

"Stop here," Esteban said.

Julio drew lines.

"There, the white house on the right."

"Are you sure?" Don Victor asked.

"I saw him there myself. The question is, how do we take him?"

"We let him come to us."

"How do we do that?"

"Watch." Don Victor scratched a short note. He handed it to Esteban.

I have information. Come out to the carriage.

E. Chorus

Esteban smiled. "So simple." He folded the note. "Julio, deliver this to Señor Longstreet at that white house."

Julio drove up the block and parked in front of O'Rourke House. He climbed down from the carriage, opened the gate, and passed up the walk to the porch. Don Victor and Esteban watched from the carriage. Both drew their guns. The woman, silhouetted in lamplight, answered Julio's knock. She shook her head and said something to the offered note. Julio shrugged. She closed the door. He returned to the carriage.

"Señor Longstreet is no there."

"Now what?" Esteban said.

"We let him come to us."

"He's not here."

"She is."

"So simple."

"Bueno."

Another knock sounded at the front door. *Now what?* Maddie wiped flour from the bread dough on her apron, crossed the dining room, and opened the door. A tall dark gentleman with jet-black wavy curls smiled.

"I am told you may have a room to rent."

"I may. Who told you?"

"Señor Longstreet."

"Funny, Beau didn't mention it."

"May I come in?"

She hesitated. Stepped back. His cloak swept around her head, a sharp blow plunged her in darkness.

Chapter Twenty-Two

She awoke sometime later. Her head ached. She was blindfolded, tied, and gagged. The clip-clop rock and sway told her she was lying on the floor of a carriage. She remembered the dark stranger. *Why? What could he possibly want with her?*

Muffled voices. She couldn't make out what they said. Spanish it sounded like. The carriage rolled on. Time passed. Her bonds cut her wrists and ankles. She wanted to scream. She needed to cry. Whoever they were, she'd not give them the satisfaction.

"How do you wish to play this out?" Esteban asked.

"We will hold the woman at Chorus's hacienda long enough for this Longstreet to find she is missing. Then you will go on to Pueblo. There you will inform the sheriff where to find the woman the Great Western Detective League is seeking. That will bring this Longstreet to us. Julio and I will be waiting for him. From Pueblo you will take the train to Topeka and discharge the obligations of our contract there."

"So simple."

"Simplicity, a sign of true genius."

Manitou Springs

Longstreet led the way up the winding trail dotted in cedar, rock falls, and sage. The trail crested the mesa. He drew rein and lifted his chin across the plain.

"If you didn't know to look for it, you'd just as well miss it."

120

"Quite a place," Cane said. "Hidden in plain sight."

"Privacy secured by nature."

"Not so private the Don's assassin couldn't find it. Lead on. Let's see who's home."

They rode in and stepped down. Longstreet banged the heavy knocker on the double wooden door. Someone had managed to remove the bloodstains from the plaza stone. The door creaked open to Eli Chorus himself. Longstreet tipped his hat.

"Mr. Longstreet, to what do I owe this unexpected surprise?"

"Afternoon, Mr. Chorus. This is my partner, Briscoe Cane. May we come in?"

"Of course." Chorus stepped aside. The cavernous foyer cooled the mountain sun.

"Can I offer you a refreshment? I'm afraid I'm a little shorthanded at the moment."

"Don't trouble yourself. We'll make this intrusion brief."

"Intrusion? Far from it. Your associate, Mr. Cane, on his last 'intrusion' saved me from an assassin's bullet."

"So he tells me."

"I'm more than grateful. What can I do for you this time?"

"We believe the man your would-be assassin worked for may be in the area. He's Mexican, patrician in bearing," Longstreet said. "He is traveling with two other men, one perhaps a Spaniard. Has anyone of that description been by?"

"Oh, dear, you don't suppose they could be intent on finishing the job, do you?"

"It's certainly possible. You haven't seen anyone then?"

"I'm afraid not, or perhaps I should say I'm pleased to say no. Are you sure of your information?"

"Our source is quite reliable."

"Are you armed, Mr. Chorus?" Cane asked.

"As a rule, no."

"Since you are 'shorthanded' I suggest you take the precaution. Our suspect may have some other mischief that brings him this way, but I wouldn't advise you take any unnecessary risks."

"Sound advice," Longstreet said.

"I shall take it as such."

"If you do catch sight of them, you can reach us at our Denver office." Longstreet handed him a card.

"Thank you both. I appreciate your concern."

"Good day, sir."

"And good day to you both."

Outside, they collected their horses, stepped into the saddle, and squeezed up a lope to the mesa trail. Longstreet checked Yankee to a walk as they wound their way back to the main road to Denver.

"Odd," Longstreet said.

"It is. They should have been here with the head start they had."

"Should have. If the Don's not here to finish Chorus, what's he here for?"

Cane had no ready answer for that. "Unless . . ."

"Unless what?"

"Unless he had vengeance on his mind."

"Vengeance?"

"He called the ferret you killed his son. Whether he is or not, the old man thought of him that way. If that's it, we best watch your back."

"Now there's a happy thought."

"Just lookin' out for you is all I'm sayin'."

Denver

Longstreet and Cane arrived in Denver too late to go to the office. They stabled the horses and parted company, Cane to the Silver Slipper, Longstreet walked home. He turned onto the tree-lined lane. Up the block O'Rourke House stood brightly lit against the early evening gloom.

He sensed it the moment he opened the door. Something was wrong. No cooking smell came from the kitchen.

"Maddie?"

Mrs. Fitzwalter emerged from the parlor, eyes red rimmed, her properly bound hair disheveled. "Oh, Beau, thank heavens you're here."

"Where's Maddie?"

"They . . . they took her."

"Took her. Who? Where?"

"Last night. Two men, I think. I was upstairs in my room. I heard a commotion. By the time I got downstairs they were loading her into a carriage. They climbed in and drove off. She didn't come home."

"A carriage? The two men, what did they look like?"

She shook her head. "It was dark. They were no more than shadows. Big though."

"Did you notify the police?"

"I did. When she wasn't back this morning. They're combing the city, but so far they've found no sign of her. Who could have done such a thing?"

A carriage. Big men. His gut gathered a sour ball. Don Victor had taken a hostage before. Samantha that time. We'd known where to find her. This was different. This was Maddie. Where could she be?

"I think I know who. The question is where?"

"But why?"

"The assassin I shot. He was part of a crime ring. The man he worked for wants revenge. I suspect they came here looking for me. When I wasn't here, they took Maddie to get at me."

He turned to leave. "We'll find her, Abigail. Keep the door locked."

"Where are you going?"

"To the police."

CHAPTER TWENTY-THREE

O'Rourke House
1910

"In this very house."

Cane nodded. "Right there in that foyer they took her."

Midday sunlight filtered through the trees, dappling the hardwood in light and shadow. I tried to absorb what it must have felt like. Were it me? Were it Penny?

"Longstreet must have been beside himself with worry."

"Blame too. He was convinced they'd snatched her to get at him. He came by the Silver Slipper once he'd satisfied himself the police knew nothing. Got me out of bed, he did. I took him downstairs, bought him a drink, and listened to his story. The police searched, but found no sign of a carriage matching what little description they had. That's not to say they didn't find carriages. They did. Just not one with Maddie O'Rourke captive in it.

"It was a nasty night for Beau. There really wasn't anything we could do. They could be anywhere. Reason said he was right. They'd grabbed her to get at him. That being the case, we could count on hearing from them. It also meant she likely wasn't in any immediate danger. I'm not sure the poor boy took much comfort from that bit of reason. It sounded better than it probably was. A homicidal killer like the Don was capable of most anything. He could just as easily have taken his anger out on her with full knowledge he'd draw Beau out too."

"So, all you could do is wait."

"Pretty much, at least until the office opened the next morning. I finally went to bed. Beau stayed up all night. I couldn't convince him worryin' to exhaustion wouldn't help when the time came he could actually do something for her. Might just as well have talked to the spittoon for all the good it did. Just be thankful, boy, we live in tamer times. Less call to worry after such things."

"Oh, I don't know, the papers are full of criminal reports every day."

"Not if you don't read 'em."

"You don't read the papers?"

"Bein' a newspaper man and all, I s'pose that's a hard hearin' for you, but no."

"Why?"

"A man comes by his own problems in life. Who needs to borrow on the anxieties of others?"

"But don't you feel the need to be informed?"

"Informed of what?"

"Events, the news."

"At my age all that ain't so important anymore. Young feller like you with your life ahead of you yet, that's different. Me? I'm just an old gumshoe detective with all his notable deeds done back there somewhere."

"That's why we're telling these stories. Men like you, Colonel Crook, Beau Longstreet, you set us up for the civil society we enjoy today. That's the way of it with history. We need to remember. We must never forget. Newspapers help us record that history. Where do you suppose I got the idea to approach the Colonel about these books in the first place? Old newspapers, that's where."

"I'm sure all that's true, so long as the papers get it right.

These days remembering my own history is about all I can muster."

Manitou Springs

Black dark inside a hood of some sort. Her arms and legs ached. She was bound to a hard wooden chair. The air was cool, musty smelling beyond the hood. She heard them lock the door to wherever they were holding her. She needed to pee. She refused to soil herself. She might have to. She refused to show fear. Who were these people? What could they possibly want with her?

Muffled footfalls sounded nearby. Keys jangled; iron clanked and clicked. A door groaned on its hinges. The door closed; someone approached, gripped the hood, and pulled it away. Lamplight blinded her. A dark shadow loomed over her. She blinked. He untied her gag. She coughed, her mouth dry as sand. He offered a dipper of water. She drank thirstily.

"Who are you? Why have you done this to me?"

He smiled. "Patrón needed you to bait his trap."

"What trap? Why me?"

"The trap is for the one called Longstreet."

"What makes you think I mean anything to him? He rents a room at my house."

"Do you kiss all those who rent your rooms? Esteban does not think so. But if you were to kiss me, things might go easier for you."

"You truss me up like a Christmas goose and then talk of kissing. I need to use the privy."

"If I release you to use the chamber pot, will you behave yourself?"

"Will you allow me to use it in privacy?"

"If you promise to behave yourself."

"I will if you will."

He laughed as he untied her bonds. "Perhaps you will decide to kiss me after all."

"I wouldn't count on it."

"Señoritas find Esteban pleasant company."

"Do you abduct all your women?"

"Only the most beautiful."

"Turn your back." She found the pot in a dimly lit corner of what appeared to be a wine cellar turned prison cell. She lifted her skirts and dropped her drawers. She half-expected him to take advantage of her when he heard the pot being used. He did not. She pulled up her bloomers and dropped her skirt.

"Do I get fed?"

"Julio will bring you a tray. If you like, I could have him bring one for me. We could find a nice bottle of wine and become better acquainted."

"If I'm to be imprisoned, I'd prefer solitary confinement."

"I only thought to help you pass the time."

"I'm sure your intentions are perfectly honorable. It's a character trait among kidnappers, I'm told."

He chuckled. "Spitfire. Esteban likes this in a beautiful woman. Give yourself a chance to like me. You would find it most agreeable."

"I'd find it agreeable if you'd let me go."

He shook his head. "I'm afraid that is not possible."

"This Patrón of yours, what does he want with Beau?"

"Why, to kill him, of course."

"What makes you think he'll come here, wherever here is?"

"Oh, he will come. I, Esteban, will see to it. Patrón will have his satisfaction. Then you will welcome my intentions toward you and I, I shall have my satisfactions too." He took the lamp, closed the door, and locked her in darkness.

Beau. They mean to kill him. Why? Will he come? He will. Will they kill him? He faces danger in his line of work. He can take care of himself. But what if . . . ?

Topeka

Atkins poured a stiff drink and settled into his desk chair haloed in lamplight at the end of a long and frustrating day. The son-of-a-bitch Palmer had a court date for his challenge to the right-of-way lease. The construction crew went out on strike. Esteban disappeared with half the money for eliminating Chorus, and the simpering little shit continues to play the merry anarchist. Now Strong says he needs a crew to cross the picket lines and break the strike. What the hell am I paying Pinkerton for? The game is getting expensive, not to mention the cost of actually building the Royal Gorge spur and its delayed river of silver profits. Strikebreakers, where do you find strikebreakers?

He drained his glass and poured another. The answer hit him as they often do, a bolt from the gloom. *Dodge.*

CHAPTER TWENTY-FOUR

Dodge City

The westbound AT&S ground to a halt at the station with a throaty blast from its whistle, amid gouts of steam and a chain of coupling clanks. Stephen Atkins stepped down to the platform from his private car. A hot breeze battered his hat. He secured it with one hand while his coat flapped in the wind. He'd need help to raise the crew Strong requested. Help he could count on and he knew where to find it.

He crossed the street east of the station. The jail occupied the adjacent corner. He expected he'd find the sheriff's office there. He'd known Bat Masterson by reputation before he actually met the man. Cool and competent in any situation, Masterson kept a lid on Ford County and a town with a volatile reputation. He may use a cane and walk with a limp, but few men who knew his reputation dared cross him. Bat made his business dealing with just the sort of men Atkins needed for this particular crew. A simple wooden sign read *Sheriff's Office* on one line, *Jail* just below. Masterson was at his desk.

He glanced up from a stack of dodgers and smiled.

"Stephen. Been half-expecting I might see you."

"That obvious, is it?" They exchanged handshakes.

"Bad news travels fast. Have a seat." He gestured to a barrel-backed wooden chair. "Not the stuffed wing chair I might find in your office, but we make do at taxpayers' expense."

"As a taxpayer, gratefully, I quite understand."

"What have you got on your mind?"

"You've heard about our labor unrest on the Royal Gorge run."

"Like I said, bad news travels fast."

"Bill Strong, my general manager, needs a crew. One prepared to cross the picket line."

"One prepared to take on the strikers you mean."

"They've only to cross the line and begin work. They will be supported by Pinkerton guards who'll maintain order."

"Like they did in Chicago?"

"I can't speak to the specifics of that situation. It was none of my business as is Pueblo none of your jurisdiction."

"I do hold that pesky U.S. marshal's shield in addition to my duties here in Dodge."

"I'd forgotten that. One never knows when that may come in handy."

"One never knows."

"Seriously now, Bat, can you help me find the men I need?"

"Hmm . . . I shouldn't be seen organizing what some might consider a mob, but I do know a man who can help you." He flicked open his watch. "Let's have a cup of coffee. We'll likely find him at the Long Branch in an hour or so. I'll introduce you."

Atkins nodded appreciatively. "Black, please."

Masterson stood. "It don't come any other way here, unless you count hot and strong."

Masterson led the way through the batwings into a subdued late afternoon crowd. Judging by the clientele Atkins sensed they'd come to the right place. He took comfort standing in the shade of Masterson's considerable reputation. Bat bellied up to the bar next to a burly fellow with a bushy red beard.

"Afternoon, Red."

"Bat." He eyed the gentleman in company with Masterson.

"Meet Stephen Atkins, Red Roach." Roach stuck out a ham-sized hand. "Mr. Atkins is looking to hire some men. I thought you might be able to help him."

"Step into my office," Roach said heading for a vacant back corner table. The bartender followed with bottle and glasses. Roach poured.

"How many men and what's the nature of the work?"

"A couple dozen should do it. The work is railroad building or more particularly crossing a Knights of Labor picket line currently preventing construction of my Royal Gorge spur."

"Heard somethin' about that." Roach aimed a tobacco stream in the general direction of a corner spittoon. "What's it pay?"

"Fifty dollars a man. A hundred for you if you raise the crew."

Roach lifted his glass. "Mr. Atkins, you got yourself a crew."

"Fifty now, the rest when it's over. I'll have a train here in the morning. Can you have your men ready by then?"

"Sure thing."

Atkins counted out fifty dollars in gold certificates. "Meet me at the depot."

Atkins and Masterson scraped back their chairs and left the saloon.

"Easier than I thought," Atkins said.

"Just got to know the right ropes."

"I'll remember that, Bat. Thanks for the help."

"No trouble."

"Easier said . . ."

Denver

Colonel Crook was surprised to find both Longstreet and Cane waiting for him to open the office. The two customarily arrived later, allowing him to catch up on any communiqués that may have come in overnight.

"Well, well, something must be afoot to get the two of you here at this hour."

"There is."

Longstreet's anxious demeanor and tired eyes were unlike him. The Colonel unlocked the door to a gray-lit inner office. He led the way to his office, scratched a match to light, and trimmed the lamp wick.

"What's the trouble?"

"It's Maddie."

"Mrs. O'Rourke? What's happened?"

"She's been abducted."

"By who? When? Where have they taken her?"

"At least two men took her night before last. Mrs. Fitzwalter was in the house at the time, but she didn't get a look at them. Briscoe and I picked up a report Don Victor was seen in Pueblo last week. We thought he might have come north to finish the Chorus job. We checked on Chorus on the ride up from Pueblo. He says he's seen no sign of any more would-be assassins."

"My gut says they took her to get at Beau," Cane said. "We know Don Victor thought highly of the ferret Beau killed. Called him his son more than once."

"Did they leave a ransom note?" Crook asked.

Beau shook his head.

Crook drummed his fingers on the desk. "I think you're on to the motive, Briscoe. They'd have no other interest in her. I doubt ransom is the motive, though I wouldn't foreclose the possibility. More likely we'll hear something. Something designed to smoke Beau here out into the open."

"So what do we do? Sit here and wait?" Longstreet paced like a caged animal.

"We can do more than wait," Crook said. "We start by notifying the League."

He scratched out an alert. He handed it to Longstreet.

"Here, take this along to Western Union. It'll give you something to do."

Pueblo

The warehouse baked uncomfortably hot in dim shadows. Men sweat and grumbled. Trevane paced, frustrated by inaction. Samantha watered strikers on the picket line while his men were left to their discomfort. The waiting, it seemed, did nothing to further the client's interest. Delay favored the strikers' objectives. Kingsley and Strong holed up in Strong's paneled caboose, watching and waiting. Time passed. The sun climbed to its zenith, beating heat on the strikers and discomfort on those awaiting their next move.

A knock sounded at the warehouse door. Trevane opened it to Samantha and her wheelbarrow. She brought water and sandwiches for the men.

"What the hell is going on out there?"

"Nothing," she said.

"I don't understand. What's Strong waiting for?"

"The other side thinks they are winning. Not O'Cairn so much, but the men do."

"What does O'Cairn think?"

"I say, I wouldn't mind hearing the answer to that one." Kingsley swung through the door.

"O'Cairn has seen this before. He knows we're here. He expects trouble."

"Does he suspect you?" Kingsley asked.

"Reggie, really? This is Samantha."

Trevane scowled.

"Right, right, I was only concerned for your safety."

"Paddy will see to it I'm out of the way before any trouble starts."

"Speaking of trouble, what the hell is going on?" Trevane

vented frustration. "What's Strong waiting for?"

"Decisive force," Kingsley said.

"What do you call this?" Trevane swept an arm over the men lounging on crates and bales.

"Strong is expecting a work crew expressly recruited to cross the picket line. They will engage the strikers and test their resolve. Should they resist, you and your men shall provide the coup de gras."

"Coup de what?"

"Gras. It's French. The grand blow."

"Hear that boys? Those axe handles are the grand blow."

"Downright regal," someone said.

Reggie raised a calming hand. "Yes, well, be patient, gentlemen. You shall all have your moment soon enough."

"When can we expect this work crew of Strong's to arrive? Samantha's visits may be refreshing, but waiting for them in a damn oven isn't."

"Strong expects Atkins will have them here soon. I shall inform you as soon as I know more."

CHAPTER TWENTY-FIVE

Pueblo

The westbound AT&S rumbled into the station belching a column of black smoke and clouds of screaming steam. Strong stood on the platform with Kingsley at his elbow. The howl of brakes faded to the clank of couplings. A blue-coated conductor opened the Pullman door and dropped a step. A red-bearded hulk stepped down, followed by a couple dozen more calloused roughnecks.

"That's our boy," Strong said.

"How can you be sure?"

The hulk strode across the platform. "Mr. Strong?"

"I am."

"Red Roach. Mr. Atkins sent me and the boys."

"We've been expecting you. This is Reginald Kingsley, Pinkerton. His Pinkerton guards will back you up in the event of trouble."

"In the event of trouble, is when we do our work," Roach said. "When do we start?"

"In the morning. We'll put you and your men up temporarily in the roundhouse just down the track there. We'll arrange some supper, but first let's get your men settled. Then you, Mr. Kingsley, and I can take a walk out to end of track and have a look at the line you'll be crossing."

"Lead the way. Come along, lads."

135

★ ★ ★ ★ ★

"They're here," O'Cairn said. He lifted his chin up the track toward the AT&S caboose.

The water girl followed his chin. "Who's here?"

"Trouble, that's who."

"How do you know?"

"See the red beard with Strong and the other suit?"

She nodded.

"There's more where the beard come from. The other suit is likely Pinkerton."

"What makes you think so?"

"It's what they do. Tomorrow, lass, I don't want you anywhere near this line."

"The men can't bear this heat without water."

"Don't argue with me. Red and his men mean to cross this line. We can't let them. When we resist, Pinkerton will move in. They mean to break us. We can't let them. It comes down to force. I'll not have your pretty head on my conscience. Understand?"

"I do. I don't like it, but I do."

"There's a good girl. Give me some time to prepare the men for what comes. Meet me in the Silver Spike for a pint in an hour."

She took her leave. *He's sweet. Trouble, but sweet.*

Samantha knocked on the warehouse door. Trevane admitted her and closed the door to stifling heat and dim light.

"Samantha, your timing is impeccable," Kingsley said. "I was just telling Trevor Strong's strikebreakers have arrived. They are prepared to cross the picket line in the morning."

"I know."

"How could that be?"

"O'Cairn spotted you and Strong looking over the line with

that bare-knuckle brawler. He put two and two together. He's preparing his men to resist. He's ordered me off the line."

"Thoughtful of him," Trevane said.

Samantha lifted an amused brow.

"Very well then, Trevor, we know they plan to resist. Have your men prepared to support Strong's crew as the situation dictates."

"How do we tell who's who?"

"Ah ha. Good point. I shall have Strong instruct the men to wear red armbands. Will that suffice?"

"It should."

"Since I'm ordered off the line, what should I do?" Samantha said.

"Stand down I should think," Kingsley said.

"All right, but first I'm to have 'a pint' with O'Cairn."

"A pint," Trevane said. "You seem to enjoy this assignment."

She patted Trevor's cheek with a half-smile. "Duty calls."

The Silver Spike was uncommonly quiet in the early evening. O'Cairn sat alone at a back-corner table wrapped in light and shadow. Samantha's Mary Miller approached the table. His eyes, somber with tension, softened at the sight of her. He stood and offered a chair.

"Quiet," she said.

"Before the storm." He signaled the bartender for beer.

"You're sure it will come to that?"

"I am. Seen it many times."

"Why do you do it?"

He paused. The bartender set frosty mugs on the table.

"The men. Usually it's the men ask us to help them."

"Usually? Not this time?"

"Nay, this time powerful people pay." He took a swallow of beer.

"And tomorrow it comes to violence. Is it worth it?"

"Worth it to whom? My superiors? Aye. The one payin'? If it weren't, he wouldn't be payin', now, would he?"

"Is it worth it to the men?"

"If we win."

"But you don't expect to win."

He sought her eyes for the pain in his. "No."

"The men think they can win. You lead them and you know they can't."

"It's me job. I did'na say I'd be proud of it."

"You surprise me, Paddy O'Cairn. I took you for an honorable man. Why would you lead a cause you know to be lost?"

"Like I said, 'tis me job."

"There are other jobs for a man of honor."

"What would you have me do, lass?"

"Call it off. Tell the men the truth. Spare them the bloodshed."

"I can'na. The Knights would nay have any respect if I did."

"You mean it'd be bad for business."

"Just like that."

"So, it is a business then. It's not about righting wrongs done the working man."

" 'Tis that too."

"So long as it's good for business."

"You've got a lot of opinion for a water girl."

"Only one that matters."

"What's that?"

"The one that stops the bloodshed."

"It can no be helped."

"It can no be helped. And when the damage is done, what then?"

He shrugged. "I've a new assignment in Chicago."

"Just like that."

He nodded.

She sat back, holding his eyes. She unfastened the red bandanna holding her hair. She slid it across the table.

"What's this?"

"For you. Hang on to it. You may need it to staunch the bleeding. Thanks for the beer."

CHAPTER TWENTY-SIX

Golden sun spars speared the horizon, turning thin wisps of cloud pink. Dark shadows emerged out of the dawn shimmer.

"Here they come, lads." O'Cairn squinted to count as they came. *Twenty or so.* "We outnumber them, lads. Hold your ground."

The men formed ranks, shoulder to shoulder, across the tracks, their signs abandoned for stout handles turned to clubs. Grim determination lined grizzled, weathered features.

Dawn light fired the red-bearded hulk centering the opposing line. Each man carried the handle to some tool, a spade, an axe, a sledge. They halted at twenty paces.

Trevane threw open the warehouse door, holding his men in readiness.

"Yo, the line," the red beard said. "Stand aside and let me crew pass."

" 'Tis a legal strike by a properly elected union of workers. Ye shall not cross our line."

"We've been hired by the rightful owner of this line to complete its work. Now stand aside."

"What say lads, do we yield?"

A chorus of *no* rose in the still morning air.

"On me, men." Red started forward, axe handle at the ready. He took the point of a loosely formed wedge, advancing on the picket center.

It struck O'Cairn in a word, *why*? Each man approaching

wore a red bandanna on his arm. He felt the water girl's scarf in his pocket as the red beard pushed his way through the center of his line. The striker fell back a step, collected himself, and swung his club for the red beard's head.

Red parried the blow and counter-stroked his axe handle, splitting the striker's scalp in a bright red gash. Blood spurt from the wound as both lines exploded in a melee of clubs and fists.

The strikers' superior numbers enveloped their attackers. Roach had chosen his men wisely. They were brawlers pit against laborers. They fought with a ferocity the strikers failed to muster. With the red bands surrounded, Trevane took it for his signal to advance. He led his men forward from the warehouse. They fell on the strikers from behind, bashing bleeding skulls to unconscious submission. Trevane hung back, searching the mob for O'Cairn.

O'Cairn saw the Pinkerton advance from the rear fringe of the brawl. He'd expected it. The fortune of numbers reversed. Strong must be made to pay for this. The time had come. With silent thanks to the water girl, he tied her scarf to his arm and slipped away from the riot.

Slowly, painfully the strikers were beaten back. Determination sapped by relentless bludgeoning. Red marshaled his men through the line, the strike breached. Battered and bleeding men littered the tracks.

Strong and Kingsley watched from the forward platform of the office caboose. Strong shook his head.

"Foolish waste. Simple men chose to follow an idealistic rabble-rouser. Did they not know they couldn't possibly win?"

"It would seem so," Kingsley said.

"Fire!" Someone shouted off to the north.

Strong cut his gaze to the alarm. Black smoke billowed just up the street. "The warehouse!" He jumped down from the car and ran up the track toward town.

Kingsley climbed down, following briskly at his heel.

"Fire brigade!" Strong waved Red and his men toward the warehouse.

Smoke and flame engulfed the combustible stores in the trackside warehouse. A shadow slipped away down an alley bound for Chicago by way of Manitou Springs.

Trevane scoured the litter of injured, searching for the labor organizer.

Kingsley reached his elbow. "I say, Trevor, have your men throw in with Strong's bucket brigade."

"Where in hell did he go?"

"Who?"

"O'Cairn."

Kingsley shrugged. "I should think he is no longer of consequence. The loss of that warehouse is."

"Funny it should catch fire just now. Come on, boys! Lend a hand over here."

Morning sun turned the hotel lobby an amber glow. Kingsley and Trevane waited. Samantha descended the stairs. Trevane looked a little the worse for wear after a long day and night. Reggie led the way to the hotel dining room. They were shown to a bright window table. A waiter in a starched white jacket poured coffee. Kingsley requested his usual tea. They ordered bacon and eggs with a side of flapjacks for Trevor.

"Too bad about the warehouse," Kingsley said.

"Little could be done to save it," Trevane said.

Samantha took a sip of her coffee and listened.

Kingsley blew steam at the rim of his cup. "Any sign of our union friend attempting to pull his men together again?"

"I stopped by the Silver Spike last night to check on that possibility. Other than sore heads drowning their sorrows in beer, I saw nothing. O'Cairn seems to have disappeared."

"He was nowhere among the bloody dregs of the riot then, was he?" Kingsley said.

"No, he wasn't. I saw him when my men first joined the fracas. Once we had the situation in hand, I looked for him. He must have slipped away soon after we came on the scene."

"Just before the warehouse caught fire," Kingsley said, turning his mustache.

"That very thought crossed my mind on the bucket brigade."

The waiter arrived with their breakfasts.

"You're awfully quiet, my dear," Kingsley said. "Any idea what might have become of O'Cairn?"

"Afraid not. We ran out of things to say when I couldn't talk him out of leading his men to certain defeat."

"You didn't tell him what to expect, did you?"

"Of course not. He knew. He said as much."

"Seems rather a waste, doesn't it?" Reggie dabbed his mustache with a napkin.

"We got paid. The Knights of Labor got paid. The workers got their heads bashed and the railroad will prosper. All's right with the world."

"Until the next time," Trevane said.

Samantha lifted a brow. "Until the next time."

"So where does that leave us?" Trevane said.

"It leaves you and your men here along with Samantha to make certain the labor disturbance doesn't reassert itself. It leaves me on the next stage to Denver. I shall file our report to head office."

Kingsley caught the afternoon stage to Denver. Trevor stalked the town, the end of track worksite, and the Silver Spike, looking for any sign of labor trouble. Samantha treated herself to a bath, a nap, and turning herself out to stunning effect in time to meet Trevor for drinks and dinner. The hotel lobby warmed to a golden glow when she made her entrance. A simple gray frock with a tempting lace bodice set off her gleaming black hair and violet eyes.

"Lilacs," he said by way of greeting.

All of it, she gathered, had the desired effect. She took his arm to a corner of the dimly lit salon. They ordered sherry.

"I wonder how long Kingsley will have us cooling our heels here?" Trevor asked.

"What, no sign of further union trouble?"

"Nary an unsubstantiated rumor."

"And there won't be."

The waiter arrived with their drinks. Samantha lifted her glass.

"To Pueblo."

"There is that."

"That what?"

"The pleasure of your company."

"There is, isn't there." She touched the rim of her glass to his and took a swallow.

"How can you be so sure?" Trevor asked.

"Sure of what?"

"That there won't be any further union trouble."

"O'Cairn's on his way to Chicago."

"And how would you know that?"

"He told me. I suspect he left town right after he set fire to the warehouse."

"You seem to have gotten along quite well with your . . . assignment."

She smiled. "Jealous?"

"Why do I bother?"

"If you must know, Paddy O'Cairn was sweet. Something of a bad boy, but sweet."

"Bad he was. Why didn't you tell Kingsley?"

"What, and get sent back to Chicago when there is Pueblo?"

"You'll have to go back eventually."

"By way of Denver. Until then . . . there's Pueblo."

Trevane warmed to her drift. "There is, isn't there."

"That's better. You're sweet, Trevor, dear. A bit slow at times but sweet."

"Sweet. I dared hope for something a trifle more rugged than that."

"What's wrong with sweet?"

"I don't know. It just doesn't sound very . . . you know."

"Nothing with sweet a little bad wouldn't spice."

"Bad, now that sounds better."

"Of course it does. My point exactly," she said with a twinkle in her eye.

Playful. She has a game afoot. "What's to be done about that?"

"I might teach you."

"You might?"

"I might."

"Where do we begin?"

"With some supper and another glass of sherry."

"Do I have to burn down a warehouse first?"

She laughed.

CHAPTER TWENTY-SEVEN

Denver
1910

Friday nights we capped off the work week with ice cream sundaes, Penny her usual caramel, me my favorite fudge. We ritually exchanged spoonsful, blending the flavors in a tasty prelude to our good-night kisses.

"That is good," I said of her caramel.

"Wildflowers," she said in reply.

"Wildflowers?"

"Yes. I think wildflowers would be nice for the wedding, don't you?"

"If it pleases you, I think wildflowers would be lovely." I'd learned to agree in such matters as it was the only response safely acceptable.

"I've narrowed the list of possibilities, but I simply cannot decide."

Uh-oh. Questions such as these could not be answered by simple agreement. It was certain to require something more. Something more that must of necessity force me to tread in uncharted territory. I waited, apprehensive.

"I definitely favor blue blooms on a white bed. What do you think?"

"Definitely blue blooms on a white bed." Dodged one there, though I had no idea what she meant by a "white bed."

"I've narrowed the choices for bedding to yarrow or daisies."

Yarrow and daisies rule out bedsheets. "Both have their place, depending on the blooms." I felt myself coming to some mastery of noncommittal ambiguity.

"I thought so too. Isn't it wonderful how much we think alike?" She favored me with one of her Mona Lisa's that never failed to set my heart a flutter and my mind a wobble.

"It is."

"The blooms of course are the problem."

"Of course." Here we go down a path from which there is no escape.

"I've narrowed the choices to columbine, larkspur, and lupine."

"I can see your dilemma. They're all lovely."

"So, which do you prefer?"

And there it is, the death knell of indecision. My mind flailed for a back door.

"All three have long and delicate blossoms. I should think any one of them might rest more comfortably on a bed of yarrow. Daisies might be over-bloomed." I have no idea where that came from. Desperation bred of panic?

Her jaw dropped. "Why, Robert, you're so clever. I hadn't thought of that. You're absolutely right. Yarrow it is. Which brings us back to the blooms."

I may have gained a point, but clearly, I'd bungled escape. One last side door to the dilemma crossed my fevered brain.

"Is there a particular significance or symbolism to any of them that might single that bloom out over the others?"

She knit her brow. "I'm not sure I know what you mean."

"Flowers sometimes are ascribed symbolic or sentimental meanings. Perhaps one of your choices speaks to something of special significance to us."

"I never thought of that. You're so romantic. I shall have to look into that aspect of the decision."

I beamed a sigh of relief. Without a ghost of a notion as to how, I'd managed to sidestep a disagreeable decision, and gain favor for the clever romantic way in which I'd accomplished it. Were I a gambling man, I should have drawn to an inside straight. We finished our caramel and fudge flavored kisses for the hand in hand walk to her home.

O'Rourke House
1910

Saturday found me arriving at O'Rourke House in time for my meeting with Briscoe. Angela responded to my knock; and as had become our custom, we exchanged pleasantries in her bright, cozy parlor while we waited for Briscoe to descend from his room.

"So, how are the wedding plans progressing?"

Women, it seems, have an insatiable appetite for information on such matters.

"Penny charts our course. I'm merely called upon in matters where needed, though I'll not pretend to be of considerable much help. At the moment she's occupied with wildflowers."

"Wildflowers!" She clapped her hands and smiled. "What a wonderfully novel idea and so much beautiful symbolism to choose from."

"There is?"

"Oh my, yes."

"I'm pleased to hear that. She's in a bit of a quandary over her final choices. I suggested she might look into symbolism for some significance, though I admit I have no knowledge of such matters."

"Well, you've set her on a fruitful path, Robert. I'm quite certain she will find useful meaning to guide her decision. And never fear, your secret is safe with me."

"I'm grateful for that. She thinks me a clever romantic for the suggestion. I rather enjoy that. Are you versed in these symbolisms?"

"More than a few. What is she considering?"

"Columbine, larkspur, and lupine."

"Oh, yes. Very good choices. Columbine is dedicated to the goddess of love, Freya. She is Patróness of fertility and . . ." She colored. "Fertility will do. Larkspur symbolizes first love. That could be most appropriate. Two good choices there."

"What about lupine?"

"Merriment and joy, another good one."

A stair creaked. "What merriment and joy?"

"Wedding flowers, Briscoe. You wouldn't understand."

"No, I suppose not."

"Well, Robert, I think you shall be symbolically well served by whatever her choice."

"I'm sure, though I'm not sure there is much in symbolism to recommend one over the other. I fear we may remain run aground on indecision."

"You underestimate women's intuition, young man. One of those blooms will speak to your Penny. You'll see. Now I shall leave you two to the nasty business of Maddie's abduction."

Briscoe led the way to the parlor with an amused look in a watery gray eye.

"How are those wedding plans coming?"

"I wish I knew. I feel a helpless rider on the coattails of chaos."

"That bad?" He took a seat.

"Perhaps I exaggerate, but I can't say I can say much coherent in the matter."

"I've not had the pleasure, but having lived as long as I have, I've observed. It's good to know when you're not needed."

"I'm well aware of that. If only my Penny were to see it that way."

"You'll get through it. Likely get used to it too. Now, where were we?"

I consulted my notes. "Maddie's abduction."

"Ah, yes." His eyes drifted.

CHAPTER TWENTY-EIGHT

Manitou Springs

Time went lost in the dark. Day and night had no meaning. The dark was interrupted by periodic feedings, provided by her tall dark captor. He'd made no move to ill-treat her, but the look in his eye when he regarded her revealed his thoughts. It made her uncomfortable. She refused to surrender to fright, but had no answer for what she might do if he were to attempt to have his way with her.

Beau. Where could he be? Would he come for her? He would if he could. How might he find her? They'd tell him. They would. The only possible reason for these men to take her was to get at him. She felt the pawn in some game, the rules for which she did not understand. She did understand the look in her captor's eye. She shivered.

They sat at Chorus's expansive dining table. Don Victor, Chorus, and Esteban gathered around one end with Don Victor at the head. Julio served.

The Don raised his glass. "My compliments, Señor Chorus, an excellent madeira."

Chorus nodded. "We make the best of our secluded circumstances."

"I too appreciate privacy."

"About our arrangement, when do you expect to complete our contract?"

The Don carved a forkful of beef. "I have given that some thought. Our other business must feed off of our next move."

"The woman?" Chorus asked.

"Sí. We need time for our adversary to spread the net in which we will catch my son's murderer. The time has come. Esteban is known to your Señor Atkins. Atkins will receive his visit. That will conclude our contract. You may depart for Topeka in the morning."

"Sí, Patrón."

"You will return to Pueblo. Notify the sheriff there the woman the Great Western Detective League seeks may be found in Manitou Springs. That will be enough to bring the one called Longstreet here. From Pueblo take the train to Topeka and see to Señor Atkins's final arrangements."

"Will you not need me to deal with Longstreet?"

"Julio and I will see to it. I will handle his execution personally. It is a blood oath. It is a blood debt. It will be slow and painful. A fitting avenging of my son's murder."

"What of the woman?" Esteban asked.

"What of her?"

"What will you do with her?"

"Eliminate her. She is of no further use."

"To you."

Carnicero turned, a dark twinkle in his eye. "She is of use to you?"

"I might enjoy that."

"Then she is yours, once you discharge the obligations of our contract to Señor Chorus."

"Gracias. Now, if you will excuse me, I will feed her and impart the joyous news of our impending union."

"Bueno. When the señor's contract is complete."

"Sí, Patrón."

★ ★ ★ ★ ★

Keys rattled the lock. Lamplight parted the darkness. She blinked. He filled the doorway, holding a tray.

"Supper is served." He offered the tray.

"How long am I to be held like this?"

"Not much longer. I must leave for a few days. When I return, we will make a more comfortable arrangement."

"I don't want an arrangement. I want to go home."

"That will not be possible. Your purpose here will be finished once your Longstreet comes for you. Once he has been dealt with, you serve no further purpose here."

"Then there is no reason to hold me."

"Oh, but there is. There are only two choices for you. You can come with me, or choose the same fate as Longstreet. Think of it while I am gone. I assure you I am the far more desirable choice of the two. Now, eat your supper."

She threw the tray at him. He ducked.

"Not hungry? You will be. Think hard. You have a choice. Pleasant or final."

He closed the door to darkness.

Don Victor and Chorus took cognac and cigars in the library after supper. The Don admired the financier's book collection, walking the cases before taking his seat.

"You have amassed a fine library. One similar to the one I had in Santa Fe."

"Had? What became of it?"

"Dynamited by operatives of this Great Western Detective League and Pinkerton agents, I believe."

"They destroy libraries?"

"I believe they would term it a regrettable consequence of my apprehension."

"Apprehension for an assassination?"

153

"A mining incident. We obtained rather substantial investments in a worthless diamond mine. Our investors were less than satisfied."

"You are a man of many talents it would appear. And you somehow managed to avoid incarceration."

"Not completely."

"You escaped?"

"My lawyers can be . . . persuasive."

"I see. And do you offer other services besides murder and diamond mine fraud?"

The door knocker sounded a sharp rap. Julio scuttled off to answer.

"You are expecting someone?" Don Victor asked.

Chorus shrugged.

The Don drew his gun. "A precaution."

Julio returned. "A Señor O'Cairn, says he is a Knights of Labor organizer and that you are expecting him."

"Ah, I suspect news of the strike." He turned to Don Victor. "I should see him."

The Don scowled. No sense attracting unnecessary attention. "I'll step into the dining room. Dispose of your business quickly."

"Send him in," Chorus said.

O'Cairn presented himself moments later. The financier greeted him alone. A second snifter on a side table picked at his curiosity.

"Have you news for me?"

"The strike is broken."

"Unfortunate you couldn't hold out longer."

"They brought in strikebreakers backed by Pinkerton agents. We were badly outnumbered. Nevertheless we delayed them. The strikebreakers will not build the spur. AT&S is in need of a crew that will. I've come for the balance of our fee."

Chorus knit his brow. "We agreed, I believe, on a somewhat longer delay."

"We got what we could. Chicago may become unpleasant if you fail to fulfill our bargain."

"Am I to take that as a threat?"

"Sound advice."

Dispose of your business quickly. Chorus went to his desk. He made out a draft in the amount of twelve thousand dollars, payable to the Knights of Labor. He handed it to O'Cairn.

"I'd say it was a pleasure doing business with you, but we spilled a lot of blood over this."

"Such things can become untidy. Now, if you don't mind, I believe we are finished. Julio, show Mr. O'Cairn to the door."

Don Victor reappeared at the sound of the front door closing. He tucked his gun back into a shoulder holster. "The Knights of Labor?"

"Business. You were about to tell me other services you might offer besides fraud and murder."

"Sí. We have been known to liquidate valuable stolen property and to provide protection against unfortunate losses for a price."

"You provide assurance?"

"We provide protection. Why do you ask?"

"Among my interests, I sometimes have needs. The Knights of Labor suited my purposes with the AT&S railroad. A timely accident might also have sufficed. Might your organization have facilitated something of that sort?"

The Don swirled his cognac, sniffed, and smiled. "Accidents? For a price."

"And your clients, they are assured of your absolute discretion?"

"But of course. In some cases, we don't even know who the client is, though that is the exception. We prefer to know. It aids in collection should the need arise. It seldom does. Those who

engage El Anillo have the capacity to pay. They are rich, powerful, even politicos. They all understand our terms are final."

"And if I were to call on you, how might I reach you?"

"You don't. You telegraph El Anillo El Paso and we will reach
you."

"How efficient."

"Sí. We are eminently efficient as you shall soon see."

CHAPTER TWENTY-NINE

Pueblo

Esteban wrestled with the manner of notifying the Pueblo sheriff of the woman's presence in Manitou Springs without exposing himself. The answer fell to him at the depot. He purchased a ticket to Topeka and boarded the next train, satisfied his part in what followed would be far removed from detection.

The telegram arrived anonymously. Pueblo Sheriff Henley Price scanned the foolscap. It appeared to shed light on the whereabouts of the woman abducted in Denver. It made no ransom demand. Who would send this to him and why? He had no answer for that. With Manitou Springs beyond his jurisdiction, all he could think to do was notify Colonel Crook.

Denver

Crook tore open the telegram and read. Finally a break.

"Beau, Briscoe, looks like we got a break."

Longstreet crossed the office in three strides followed by Cane.

"What have you got?"

Crook handed him the telegram.

"Manitou Springs."

"Manitou Springs?" Cane asked.

"Henley Price got a tip. Maddie is somewhere in Manitou Springs."

" 'Somewhere' narrows down pretty fast in this case," Cane said.

"Chorus, but why? How does that make sense?"

"If Don Victor and his men grabbed her, why would they take her there?" Cane mused.

"To kill him? They didn't when you thought that's what they were there for," Crook said.

"Maybe they wanted me first, figuring they could catch up with Chorus when they got to it," Beau said.

Cane nodded. "When they missed you, they grabbed Maddie to get to you. They take her to Chorus's mountain mansion hideout, finish their contract on him, and set a trap for you."

"Two birds with one stone," Crook said.

"Come on," Beau said.

Cane looked to Crook. The boss nodded. An hour later they were on the trail south.

Manitou Springs

Longstreet drew rein on the narrow mountain trail below the mesa crest. He stepped down and left Yankee to crop. Cane took his lead, leaving Smoke to graze.

"How do you want to play this?" Cane asked.

"I've been chewing those oats on the way down here. They'll be waiting for us. The tip Sheriff Price got wasn't left by some Good Samaritan. They planted it to lure us in. More particularly to lure me in. Best I can come up with is to give 'em what they expect, me. I'll ride in. I'd like to keep one card in the hole."

"That would be me."

"That would be you."

"S'pose you get killed before I get to you."

"You'd make a damn poor hole card then, wouldn't you?"

"And you'd make one dead poker player."

"So, here's what we're gonna do. Wait here until dark. You

circle around to the back of the mansion and figure some way in. I'll ride in when you're ready."

"How are you gonna know when I'm ready?"

"Got a match?"

"You'll never see a match from here."

"Oh, no?" Longstreet rummaged in a saddlebag and drew out a worn telescope. "War souvenir."

"That just might see a match."

Longstreet extended the tube and fitted it to his eye. He scanned the house and handed the telescope to Cane.

"See the tree line behind the house?"

Cane squinted. "Yeah."

"Nice dark background. See the back corner of the house?"

"Um-hum."

"Strike your match there."

Cane collapsed the tube. "Then what?"

"You get inside while I ride in."

"How do you get in?"

Longstreet shrugged. "I knock on the front door."

"Just like that."

"Just like that. How else are they going to know to let me in?"

"Silly me. After that?"

"Ball goes up and the cotillion begins with a reel."

"Cotillion. Never would have guessed."

Early evening draped the mansion in blue mountain shadow. Cane picketed Smoke, then checked his guns and blades while he waited for full darkness to fall.

"It's time," Cane said. "Look for a match at the northeast corner in about an hour."

Longstreet checked his watch and nodded.

"Good luck," Cane said.

"You too. You're my ace in the hole."

"Hope that hole ain't six foot deep."

Shadows swallowed him up.

Rumpled running cloud cover gave the ground patches to light the way. Cane gave the mansion a wide berth to the south and east before working his way to the back. Lamplight lit a kitchen window at the back of the house toward the west end. Nearby Cane found what he hoped for, the door to a cellar. Even better, an unlocked cellar. He lifted the door and peered into musty, inky black. He opened one half of the double door until it lay silently on the ground. A step creaked under his boot on the way down. He froze. No sound. A sliver of light across the gloom signaled another door. He snapped a lucifer to light and made his way through stores of smoked meat, canned goods, burlap sacks, dried beans, and peppers. He flicked out the match and tested the door handle. It too was unlocked. Satisfied he'd gained entry he returned to the night air and made his way to the northeast corner of the building.

The hour passed agonizingly slow. Longstreet's gut knotted with worry and frustration. He watched the hands of his watch creep toward the moment he could actually do something. Something he hoped would bring Maddie back to him. Time. He extended the telescope and fit the piece to his eye, staring into the darkness across the mesa. A match flared a pinprick of light in the lens. Longstreet collapsed the tube and pulled back from the ledge. He checked his gun. The .38 Colt Lightning he customarily carried in his shoulder rig felt light for what might lay ahead. *Maddie, I'm coming.* The thought gnawed at his gut on the ride down from Denver. It had near finished his insides in the last hour's wait. He strapped on a holster with a heavier .44 Colt, comforted by the heft on his hip. He stowed the telescope in his saddlebag, collected Yankee's reins, and stepped into the saddle. He squeezed up a lope to the crest of the mesa.

Lights shown in first floor windows he remembered for a parlor, a dining room, and a room he'd not seen further to the rear beyond the dining room. He drew rein at the broad veranda and stepped down. He lifted the hammer thong on the Colt and climbed the steps.

He banged the brass door knocker. Moments later bootheels clipped the polished wood beyond. The door swung open to a sinister, dark featured hulk he'd not seen on either of his earlier visits. It served to confirm his suspicions.

"Is Mr. Chorus in?"

The brute stepped back holding the door. "I will tell him you are here."

"No need, Julio." Don Victor stepped out of the parlor, gun leveled. "We've been expecting you, Señor Longstreet."

"We meet again, Don Victor."

"Sí. On my terms this time. Julio, get his guns,"

The giant peon took Longstreet's guns.

"Now if you don't mind, step into the parlor and take the seat of honor."

Longstreet followed the Don's gun muzzle into a large room brightly lit by a crystal chandelier. A sturdy wooden chair stood in the center of the room. Longstreet glanced over his shoulder.

"The seat of honor?"

"Do you see another? Remove your coat and sit!"

Longstreet shrugged off his coat. "Where's Maddie?"

"We shall bring her to you once you are comfortably seated."

Longstreet sat.

"Bind him, Julio."

The brute tossed Longstreet's guns on a window settee and gathered lengths of stout rope. He tied Longstreet's wrists to the chair arms and his ankles to chair legs, with several secure wraps around his chest to the chair back.

"Not taking any chances you might face a fair fight. I would think the great Don Victor Carnicero might have more machismo than that."

"Silence, you impudent dog. The only sound I wish to hear coming from you are the screams of agony when the cutting begins. You shall have every chance you gave Escobar."

"A murderer."

"Silence. I have all the blood rage you need to die slowly while your woman watches. Fetch her, Julio."

The brute departed.

"What have you done with Chorus? Finished your blood money contract? Who hired you to kill him?"

"El Anillo business is none of your business. The only El Anillo business of interest to you is your death."

CHAPTER THIRTY

Cane cracked the cellar door open to a long lamplit corridor lined with doors. A stair creaked under a heavy weight at the far end of the hall. Cane ducked back. A powerfully built dark-skinned man paused at a door near the stairway. He shifted a sawed-off shotgun to one hand and shuffled a ring of keys. He fit one to the lock, picked up a lamp from a nearby table, and stepped inside. Moments later a disheveled Maddie O'Rourke stepped into the hall. Her captor returned the lamp to the table and prodded her toward the stair with the shotgun.

Cane stepped into the hall and paused. He listened to the footfalls on the stairs die away. He made his way to the end of the hall and paused again to listen. He heard indistinct voices somewhere beyond the top of the stairs. He placed a boot on one side of the bottom step and gently added his weight, hoping to avoid any telltale creak.

The brute he called Julio returned with a red-eyed, disheveled Maddie who otherwise appeared unhurt.

"Beau!" Her eyes shot round; her hand covered her mouth.

"Ah, the touching reunion." Carnicero holstered his gun and drew a razor from his coat pocket. He flicked it open and tested the edge. "Take a fond look at him my dear. Soon enough he will no longer be the pretty boy of your dreams. By the time I finish, he will beg for death to take him and you will no longer recognize what is left of him."

He hung a leather strop on the back of Longstreet's chair beside his left ear and gently stropped the razor. The air hung silent save for the soft slap of the blade.

"Where to begin?"

Maddie dropped to her knees. Tears streaked her cheeks. "Please, no."

"He should have thought of you before he killed my son."

"Your son was a cutthroat murderer. The apple doesn't fall far from the tree."

"Cut throat? No, never. Cut throat would be far too merciful for you. No, death will take you by many cuts. Many cuts, sí. I think first . . . you are right-handed, no?" He nodded at the pistol rig on the settee. "Sí, right-handed. We shall begin with the trigger finger that killed my son. Where you are going, you shall have no need of it." He dropped the strop and tested the blade. "Sí," he grinned.

Longstreet fixed the Don with a stony glare.

Maddie covered her eyes, her shoulders shaking, racked in silent sobs.

Julio stood stoic, the shotgun in the crook of his arm.

"Nobody move." Cane stepped out of the dining room, Forehand and Wadsworth leveled at Carnicero, his .44 aimed at Julio.

"Now drop the razor and set the shotgun down gently and step away from it."

No one moved.

"You first then, Carnicero." Cane cocked the spur trigger hideaway.

The Don blinked. The razor slipped from his fingers. "Do as he says."

Julio lowered the shotgun to the floor and stepped back.

"Nice you could make it," Beau said.

"Better late than never."

"Not in this case."

"Maddie, there is a knife behind my holster," Cane said. "Cut Beau loose."

Trembling, Maddie got to her feet.

"Walk around behind me to get it and then behind Beau. I wouldn't want you in my line of fire should I have to kill one of these scum."

Maddie retrieved Cane's knife and set to work on Beau's bonds.

Carnicero dropped to his knees, reaching for the pistol inside his coat.

Cane's backup spit muzzle flash before the Don could clear leather.

A bright red blossom opened the Don's chest. His eyes flashed fury. The gun wobbled in his hand.

Cane fired again.

Don Victor Carnicero's eye-light went out.

Julio dropped to the floor. The shotgun blast shattered the chandelier. Raining fire on the carpet. The brute disappeared in darkness.

Cut from his bindings Longstreet waved Maddie to the dining room.

"Help me with this, Briscoe." He began rolling up the carpet, dousing the flames.

Cane dragged the Don's body out of the way. "What about old Julio?"

"What about him. El Anillo is a serpent with its head cut off. This time there won't be any early release."

With the fire reduced to a smoldering rug, Beau turned to Maddie. "Are you all right?"

She rushed into his arms. "I am now. Oh, Beau, I was so scared."

He held her. She shook. "I'm sorry, so sorry. I never intended for you to get mixed up in anything like this."

"I didn't know what to think when they took me."

"You must have known I'd come for you."

"I hoped you would and I was afraid you would. I had no idea what that awful man was capable of."

"He's no trouble now."

She sagged against him.

He appeared in the foyer entrance to the parlor. "Once again, Mr. Longstreet, I find myself in your debt. This time for saving my home from burning down."

"Chorus! I thought you were dead."

"No, I'm very much alive, again thanks to you. A prisoner in my own home and perhaps a bit of unfinished business for our friend there, but certainly not dead."

They buried Carnicero the following morning, deciding not to subject Maddie to escorting his corpse back to Denver. They saddled up at midmorning with Maddie doubled up on Yankee with Beau. She held him tight as she had the previous night, keeping her thoughts to herself. Once clear of the narrow mountain trail and on the open road to Denver, Longstreet and Cane turned to the loose ends of the case.

"Why didn't they finish the Chorus job?" Longstreet asked.

"Good question. They'd have had the use of the house either way."

"Chorus claims he was a prisoner in his own home. Do you believe him?"

"Why would he lie?"

"Another good question. Not sure we're getting anywhere with this one. I wonder what happened to the Spaniard."

"He had to leave for some reason," Maddie said softly.

"Any idea why?"

"No."

"Do you know who he is?"

"Calls himself Esteban. He frightens me. He said I had a choice. Go with him or be killed."

"Nice fella. Don't worry. He can't hurt you anymore." He wrapped a protective arm over hers and squeezed.

"So what do you suppose this Esteban is up to?" Cane asked.

"Sending anonymous telegrams to Henley Price?"

"That makes sense. There must be more to it than that."

"What makes you think so?"

"He wasn't on our welcoming committee."

"Which brings us back to what became of him."

"It does. Do you think he's El Anillo?"

Longstreet glanced at his partner. "No way of knowing for sure, but if I were to bet, I'd bet he is."

"My gut says so too. Maybe the snake can grow a new head."

"I'd rather not think of it that way."

"Neither would I, but you can't rule it out. At least not yet."

CHAPTER THIRTY-ONE

Denver

O'Rourke House

On returning home Maddie took a bath, got a good night's sleep, and threw herself into normalcy cleaning and cooking. Longstreet saw through it. She was still deeply troubled by her ordeal. The second evening home after they did up the supper dishes, he took her by the arm and led her to the parlor settee.

"Sit down and relax. I'll be right back."

She locked her eyes in his and saw care for her there. He went to the dining room sideboard. He returned carrying two cut crystal glasses with a stout measure in each.

"The good Irish stuff," he said, handing her a glass. He sat beside her and touched his rim to hers. It coaxed a small smile.

"There, that's better. You're home. You're safe." He took a swallow.

She took his lead.

"There's more, you know."

She knit her brow and tilted her chin in her inquisitive way.

He took her glass and set them both on the side table.

"You're loved."

Her eyes glistened moist.

He kissed her, gently.

"Beau Longstreet, did I just hear what I think I heard?"

"If you heard me say 'I love you,' you did."

She traced the line of his jaw with a finger.

"There's more than that."

More? lit her gaze.

"If you'll have me, Maddie O'Rourke, will you marry me?"

"Oh, Beau." A tear welled in one eye.

"Tears? Is it that bad?"

"No, love. It's so . . . so much all at once."

"You can't think it sudden. We've been traveling this path for some time now."

"We have and I felt it too. It's only . . ."

"Only what?"

She bit her lip. "I've seen the risks in what you do. It was one thing hearing the stories. Even turning peevish over that Samantha woman. Now I've experienced it for myself."

"I'll quit if it frightens you."

"I'll not ask that of you. Let me think. Let me get used to the idea."

"Think then."

"There's more."

"There is?"

"I love you too."

"Then I think that's a good place to start thinking."

A kiss claimed them as never before.

Denver & Rio Grande Office

"Mr. Kingsley to see you, sir."

Palmer looked up from his lawyer's brief. "Send him in, Vincent."

The Pinkerton doffed his bowler and stepped into the office.

"Mr. Palmer, Reginald Kingsley, Pinkerton Agency." He extended a hand. "You sent for me, sir."

"So I did, Mr. Kingsley," Palmer said, shaking his hand. "Have a seat."

"How might Pinkerton be of service to the D&RG?"

"Direct. I like that. As you may be aware, we have a legal dispute with the AT&S over the Royal Gorge right-of-way. My attorneys now advise me we are likely to prevail in our litigation. I am also aware AT&S is approaching the mouth of the gorge at Cañon City. I want them stopped there. We've obtained a temporary injunction to halt construction until a court of competent jurisdiction can rule in the matter."

"Finish the job the labor dispute could not."

"In a manner of speaking. I'm prepared to retain Pinkerton to take the heights above the gorge and hold the AT&S to terms of the injunction. Slow construction until the courts restore our right-of-way."

"That can be arranged. As it happens, I have men in Pueblo who could take up a guard on the gorge."

"Yes, I'm aware of that. Are you willing to undertake the assignment?"

The corners of Kingsley's mustache lifted in a small smile. "You mean am I willing to change sides in the dispute? I have men for hire. You are prepared to engage them. I say when might you like us to begin?"

"How quickly can you move?"

He made a show of consulting his pocket watch. "By wire, we should hold the heights by tomorrow."

"Splendid."

Pueblo
Late afternoon light filtered a golden glow through lace curtains, warming the strewn bedclothes. Samantha drowsed. Trevane lay on his side admiring the swell of her hip. A sharp rap at the door intruded on the idyll.

"Who is it?" he called.

"Telegram for Mr. Trevane."

"Slip it under the door."

Nothing. Trevane groaned defeat. He rolled off a noisy spring and padded to his clothes. He fished two bits out of his pocket and slid the coin under the door in exchange for the wire. He tore it open.

"Trouble," Samantha breathed.

"Kingsley. We've been hired by the Denver & Rio Grande to hold the heights above Royal Gorge at Cañon City against further track laying by AT&S on D&RG right-of-way."

"I thought AT&S held the right-of-way."

"Court says they don't."

"Pity. When do we leave for Cañon City?"

"In the morning."

"At least we have that."

"I need to notify the men."

She feigned a pout. "Supper's soon enough." She smiled behind a crooked finger.

"I suppose it is." He padded to her bid.

Cañon City

Royal Gorge is a rock gash carved over the centuries by the Arkansas River. AT&S track passed Cañon City building out a three-mile run to the gorge. Trevane and his men claimed rocky heights near the mouth of the gorge where tracklayers would construct a platform to support the east end of their trestle bridge. From these impregnable positions, work crews could be held at bay for so long as the courts might require to resolve the right-of-way dispute.

From the heights, the gorge presented a formidable barrier to construction of a railroad trestle. Trevor, not being an engineer, weighed it on the side of impossible.

"They figure to span that thing with a bridge," he said to one of the men.

The man spit a stream of amber tobacco juice. "Don't see how."

"We won't either if we do our job."

"Nope."

"I have no idea how they bridge that thing. I know this much though. I wouldn't be caught dead on the crew building it, or on a train crossing it."

"Dead pretty well covers it."

With Trevor otherwise occupied, Samantha debated returning to Chicago. Still, she favored the idea of returning by way of Denver with Trevane to amuse a portion of the trip. She settled into a Cañon City hotel resigned to boredom.

CHAPTER THIRTY-TWO

Denver
1910

The following Friday found us at our usual sundae booth. Spoons in hand we scooped into our cold creamy treat. The flower question hovered in the background. We small-talked our work week's experiences. At length, I ventured into my recent triumph.

"So did symbolism assist in a flower selection?"

"I'm afraid not."

"I was afraid of that."

"You were?"

"I was. Love, first love, and joy, all of them speak to our union."

Her eyes shown misty. "You looked into it too. Oh, Robert, that's so . . . so thoughtful and romantic."

Romantic again. I left the source of my information to imagination. "I suppose that leaves us no closer to a selection."

"Not so. I've managed a preference. That is if you agree, of course."

Agree? Does ice cream melt?

"I prefer the Columbine."

Fertility. I liked the sound of that. "A lovely choice. What led you there?"

"The blooms. They're so pretty."

"They are. Columbine, it is."

On the walk to Penny's rooming house, I marveled at the tortured trail leading to our floral decision. From beds to symbolism to the simplicity of a bloom visible from the outset. I had a hunch this journey of discovery was only just beginning. Bewildered in the end I surrendered to something I understood, kissing.

O'Rourke House
1910

I arrived at the appointed hour. Angela admitted me to the mingled scents of floor polish and baking bread. She greeted me with a warm smile I suspected of eager anticipation.

"Was the symbolism helpful in reaching a decision on Penny's flowers?"

"Not really. All of them spoke to some sentiment of our union."

"Mmm . . . a plenty of good choices. I'm not surprised. Has she been able to reach a decision?"

I nodded.

"The Columbine, I'll wager."

"Why, yes. How did you know?"

"They're so pretty."

My jaw dropped at the symmetry of some logic I'd failed to grasp.

"What's pretty?" Briscoe asked as he stepped off the stairs.

"Columbine, dear," Angela said.

Dear. I had the odd sensation my head was spinning.

"Mountainside's full of them," Cane said.

"They're still pretty."

"If you say so," Cane said.

"Tell Penny she's made a fine choice, Robert. Now I shall leave you two to whatever nefarious escapade occupies you today."

She was gone on a flounce of petticoats. Cane followed her with his gaze, a half-measure of amusement in his eye.

"Come along, Robert. Let's get to it."

I followed him into the parlor and took my listening seat and proffered a bottle of his weekly stipend. Briscoe deposited it beside his chair. He smoothed his mustache in the web of thumb and forefinger.

"Let's see, what it is it we need to get to?"

I consulted my notes. "Trevane and his men secured the Royal Gorge heights."

"Ah yes, things was about to get interesting there . . ."

Topeka

Stephen Atkins paced his spacious office, half-listening to his high-priced lawyer. The news was not good.

"The appeals court overruled the lower court, awarding D&RG's prior claim on the right-of-way without setting aside the lease."

"So that's in our favor," Atkins said.

"For now. Palmer intends to appeal to the Supreme Court."

"Do you think the court will hear the case?"

"That's always hard to say. Given the economic significance of the dispute, I'd lean toward the court hearing the appeal."

"Then what do you make of our chances?"

The lawyer fidgeted in his chair, uncomfortable with speculation. "Not an easy call."

"I don't pay you to make easy calls. What do you make of our chances?"

"The appeals court acknowledges D&RG's prior claim on the merits. The court didn't rule on the lease, which renders the ruling indecisive, but did grant an injunction against further development of the right-of-way, pending a definitive ruling. At the next level the court is asked to decide the merits of Palmer's claim of breach, invalidating the lease."

"We know all that. The injunction is irksome, but at this point little more than that."

"Ignore it and you risk being found in contempt."

"I am in contempt, contempt for this whole dispute over a perfectly valid agreement. That's how the courts must certainly decide it on the merits."

"I can argue both sides on that one."

"Of course you can. You're a lawyer. In this case you're my lawyer. Which of your arguments can you win, mine or my opponent's?"

"There's a chance your argument could lose."

Atkins scowled. "Then I suggest you do some more work on my argument."

The lawyer took that for dismissal and left the office, passing Atkin's assistant at the door.

"Telegram from Cañon City."

Now what? Atkins tore open the foolscap.

D&RG Pinkerton force holding heights above gorge. Further development halted.

Strong

Pinkerton. Palmer means to stall us until the court rules. Now what? Atkins resumed his pacing. We've leased stations and facilities all along that line. We've made improvements. They're ours. I'm damn sure not going to gift wrap them for that son-of-a-bitch Palmer. Atkins caught up mid-stride. A slow smile tugged at the corners of his mouth. That just might balance things out some in our favor. He crossed to his desk and scratched out a telegram.

W. B. Masterson . . . Dodge City, Kansas.

CHAPTER THIRTY-THREE

Dodge City

Ford County Sheriff W. B. Masterson slipped into his deputy U.S. marshal's jurisdiction as he scanned Stephen Atkins's telegram. Atkins, it seemed, felt sufficiently concerned for the security of his right-of-way properties to formally request law enforcement protection. He'd turned to Pinkerton in the past, though now it appeared Pinkerton had been engaged on behalf of his rival Denver & Rio Grande. The Royal Gorge dispute was headed toward armed confrontation faster than court resolution. Clear eyed, cool headed, and dapper, Masterson considered his options. Atkins was a presence in Kansas politics. Helping him couldn't hurt a public official. The AT&S assets in question stretched from Dodge to Cañon City. It would take a good-sized posse to secure them. That he could manage. The key to controlling the right-of-way as currently constructed centered on the Roundhouse in Pueblo. Control that and all you had to do was protect the rest of the line from damage or destruction. He checked his pocket watch. Time to head down to Chalk Beeson's Long Branch to work the early evening crowd.

The early crowd bellied up to the long-mirrored bar. Masterson spotted Ben Thompson at the end of the bar. A sure hand with a gun, the Englishman and Bat had a history going back to a gun scrape in the Lady Gay Saloon in Sweetwater, Texas, following the Red River War. Bat was assaulted by a trooper in a dispute over a dance hall girl. Bat killed the trooper. The trooper accidently killed the girl with the ball ending up in Bat's pelvis, accounting for his limp. The wound put him down. Ben Thompson put his gun between the fallen Masterson and the trooper's pals. They'd been friends ever since.

"Bat."

"Ben."

"Care for a drink?"

Bat nodded.

Ben signaled for a glass and poured from his bottle. "What's up?"

"I'm raising a posse."

"For?"

"AT&S needs its line from here to Cañon City protected."

"Big job."

"It is. You in?"

"Why not. How many men do you figure to need?"

"Fifty should do it."

"How many do you have?"

"You and me."

"Good start. What about him?" Thompson tossed his head to a dealer shuffling cards at a corner table waiting for a game.

"Holliday? That disagreeable cuss?"

"He may be disagreeable but he's competent. You only have forty-eight more to go. Do you have to like them all?"

"You may be right at that."

"Don't hold your nose."

"I'll try."

Bat drifted off to Doc's table. Thin, red-eyed, and wracked with consumption, Doc Holliday hovered somewhere between scarecrow and cadaver. His suit hung on his frame like wet laundry to a clothesline on a windless day. He lifted a watery eye to his approaching visitor.

"W. B. Masterson," Doc coughed. "What brings you by, slumming?"

"I'm raising a posse."

"Does it pay?"

"Ten dollars a week and found."

"Who we after?"

"We're not. We're gonna nursemaid the AT&S from here to Cañon City."

"Lot of nursing."

"AT&S is paying."

"Why do they need nursing?"

"Right-of-way dispute with the D&RG."

"I read where the courts had that one."

"They do. Might come to gunplay before the courts settle it. You in?"

"Cards haven't been all that generous of late. I'm in. Care for a game?"

"Not unless you've got forty-seven men up your sleeve."

"There I disappoint. No more up there than two jacks."

"Aces would be gaudy."

"Tastelessly obvious," Holliday said around a belt of his everpresent whiskey.

"If you see any good ones, send 'em my way."

"I hesitate to recommend that odious fellow over there." Doc lifted the tuft of beard on his chin.

Bat glanced over his shoulder. "Dave Rudabaugh."

"Dirty Dave's more likely the object of a posse pursuit than a posse man."

"Maybe so, but he's not now. Thanks, Doc. I'll let you know when we leave."

Rudabaugh and Bat had a history. That time Rudabaugh and his gang of train robbers were the object of a Masterson posse pursuit not long after Bat was sworn in as Ford County sheriff.

A snowstorm delivered Dirty Dave and a couple of his ac-
complices into custody. When the case came to trial, Rudabaugh turned state's evidence and walked. Crossing the saloon
Bat got a sniff of Dirty Dave's well-earned reputation. Dave
caught sight of him and lifted his hands in mock surrender.

"Bat, I'm clean."

"Dave, you haven't been clean in years."

"You know what I mean."

"I'm not here to arrest you."

"There's a mercy."

"I'm recruiting a posse. Care to nursemaid some railroad assets?"

"Thought Pinkerton did that."

"They're manning the other side."

"Who's side we on?"

"AT&S. Pinkerton's got D&RG."

"Let me guess, we're going to the Royal Gorge."

"We are, along with forty-nine of my closest friends."

"Big posse. What's it pay?"

"Ten dollars a week and found. You in?"

Dave turned a filthy pants pocket inside out, exposing a hole.
"What do you think?"

"I'll let you know when we depart."

Pueblo

Three days later Masterson and fifty men left Dodge westbound
on the AT&S. Bat dropped off deputies to secure each AT&S
stop in dispute with the D&RG. He reached Pueblo ac-
companied by Ben Thompson, Doc Holliday, Dave Rudabaugh,
Luke Short, and ten others.

Short, a rancher, sometimes lawman, and gambler, lived up
to his name. A wise man didn't underestimate the grit behind
his stature. He possessed a lethal command of firearms, which

served him well on multiple occasions. He joined Thompson in the posse as true friends of Bat Masterson.

Detrained, Bat surveyed the roundhouse. It presented a fortress-like brick enclave, served by track coming and going.

"Should be easy enough to hold that," Short said.

Thompson nodded agreement.

"With a little extra fortification, we might hold off an army," Bat mused.

"What kind of fortification?" Short asked.

"Follow me."

Masterson commandeered a freight wagon for official use and set off with Short and Thompson aboard. At the west end of town, he hauled lines in front of a regional Colorado reserve armory. They climbed down from the wagon and approached a gated yard, the gate chained and locked.

"We're not gonna just walk into that place," Short said.

"No, we're not," Bat said, drawing his gun.

Short and Thompson exchanged glances.

Bat fired. The lock shattered. The gate swung open. He led the way across a small outer quadrangle. A second lock secured the heavy wooden door to a storeroom. A second shot opened the way inside. Bat scratched a match to a lantern near the door and handed it to Short. He prowled among the gun cases and powder kegs until he found the canvas tarp he sought. He pulled the tarp aside.

Thompson smiled broadly. He clapped Short on the shoulder and chuckled. "Fortification, Luke, fortification."

The Gatling gun gleamed of polished brass with a light coat of oil.

"Bring the wagon into the yard, Ben," Bat said. "We'll get this beauty and her ammunition loaded."

CHAPTER THIRTY-FOUR

Cañon City

The soft sound of a note slipped under the door intruded on the golden languor of late afternoon. She winced. *Kingsley,* her intuition said. She rolled over and glanced at the carpet. Curious, not a telegram. She slid off the bed and padded to the door. She slit the envelope with a nail.

Bored? Supper at six. Meet in the lobby.

Trevor

She smiled. Poor boy, must be lonely sweating it out atop all those rocks. He'd come down from the mountain to play a little hooky. Prospects improved, she smiled to herself.

She descended the stairs to the lobby promptly at six. The anticipation that greeted her exceeded expectations. Trevor's tongue didn't hang out, but his eyes fairly did.

"We'll what brings you off the mountain?" Transparent as it might be, she couldn't resist.

"Only the thought of you pining away in these dreary circumstances."

"So sweet of you to think of me." She patted his cheek, allowing her hand to linger a moment before offering her arm.

He led the way to Cañon City's only café with table linen. He ordered a bottle of sherry. Glasses poured, they inspected the menu. They ordered steaks, tipped a toast to tipping toasts, and settled in to enjoy an evening of diversion.

"How are things at end of track?" Samantha asked.

"Decidedly under control. Every morning the work crew approaches the site. We lob a couple of shots into the dirt, far enough in front of them no one is in danger of injury. They retreat and we roast for the rest of the day."

"For this you get paid."

"I do, though I'd much prefer something a bit less, shall we say, predictable."

Samantha lifted her half-empty glass, "Then to unpredictable." She drained it.

Trevor poured. "Any developments on the court case?"

"Nothing new. I hear Atkins has somehow managed a rather substantial U.S. marshal's presence along the line."

"Really, what on earth for?"

"To protect his interests. I suspect in anticipation the court may not decide in his favor. In that event, one never knows, perhaps you'll get your desired unpredictability."

"I was rather hoping I shouldn't have to wait for a court to decide."

"Nasty boy. The jury is out."

"Do we expect an early verdict?"

The steaks arrived.

"Court is in recess."

Denver

The court's decision rattled down the wires to Denver and Topeka in favor of the Denver & Rio Grande. Palmer grinned broadly. Now all he needed to do was evict the usurpers from his properties. He needed to engage local law enforcement up and down the line. Fortunately, he knew how to do just that. He tucked notice of the court's order in his pocket and headed for the offices of the Great Western Detective League.

Bright sunlight put a spring in his step; victory put determination in his stride. He swung into the League offices and crossed the reception area to Crook's door.

"William, what brings you by?" Crook rose with a smile.

"Afternoon, Colonel. I need a little help with pest control."

"Pest control? That seems a bit out of our line."

"Not this brand of pests."

"Very well then, have a seat. What manner of pests have infested you?"

"Atkins has marshaled occupying forces at all my fueling stations and depots east of Pueblo to Cañon City."

"You say your stations and depots. Has the dispute been settled?"

"It has. The Supreme Court ordered the right-of-way restored to the D&RG." He slid the telegram across the desk.

"I see. Have you something more official than a telegram? A court order for example."

"The paperwork will catch up to us. For now, I need your League members in the appropriate jurisdictions to prepare to serve the eviction. Can you help me, Colonel?"

"The reward?"

"Ten thousand."

"I believe that can be arranged."

"I thought it might." Palmer rose, shook Crook's hand, and departed.

Crook stepped to his office door. "Longstreet, Cane, a moment please."

Both left their desks and filed into Crook's office.

"Colonel?" Longstreet asked.

"Supreme Court decided the Royal Gorge right-of-way decision in favor of the Denver & Rio Grande. William Palmer, D&RG president, has just engaged the League to evict AT&S

security forces from the right-of-way facilities. I'll alert the affected League offices. I want you two to head down to Pueblo and give Henley Price a hand. Pueblo has the roundhouse. That's easily the most valuable asset to the line. Can you leave by morning?"

Both nodded.

"Very good."

O'Rourke House

Longstreet headed home determined to put the best face on it. A feeling hung in the air like a cool morning fog since they returned from Manitou Springs. He couldn't put his finger on it. Everything seemed normal on the surface, yet there was something in Maddie's demeanor. She wasn't aloof, reserved maybe. Leaving on assignment felt like the wrong news to bring home. Then again, maybe it was all in his head.

He stepped into foyer to warm cooking smells coming from the kitchen.

"Beau, is that you?"

"Guilty as charged." He crossed the dining room to the kitchen. Maddie stood at the stove stirring a kettle of stew, her hair swept up in curls atop her head. He slipped up behind her and kissed the nape of her neck. She shivered a little.

"You are guilty."

"Good."

"Take off your coat and relax before supper."

"Gotta pack."

"You're leaving?"

"In the morning. Briscoe and I are headed down to Pueblo. The courts have settled the Royal Gorge dispute in favor of the Denver & Rio Grande. The AT&S may need some encouragement to give up their holdings."

"Encouragement. You mean trouble."

185

"We hope not."

"Will you be gone long?"

"I hope not."

Supper passed with no further talk of travel or trouble. Beau helped clear the table and dry the dishes. Mrs. Fitzwalter took herself off to her room to read. Beau squired Maddie to the parlor settee.

"Care for an Irish?"

"Plying me with spirits, is it?"

"Not unless you want to be plied."

" 'No' might be best for clear-headed conversation."

"Where's the fun in that?"

"Beau."

"I know. You know I'm going to ask."

"I do and here you go again, off to some danger I'm left to imagine."

"It's nothing I can't handle."

"I know you can. The question I must decide is, can I?"

"So you're still thinking."

"I am."

"Love you as I do, Maddie O'Rourke, we're not getting any younger."

"Ah, I do love to hear you say that. Not the younger part of course."

"Of course. Now lest we forget the love part, consider this." He lifted her chin, took her lips in his, and imparted that which mere words could not express.

"This leads to clear-headed thinking?" she sighed.

"One can only hope."

"Addled as I am a wee drop of Irish couldn't hurt."

Beau took himself off to the dining room buffet and poured two drams. He returned to green eyes clouded with uncertainty.

He touched the rim of her glass and backed off of his quest. She needed time. He hoped that time was all she needed.

CHAPTER THIRTY-FIVE

Cane and Longstreet rode south at sunup the next morning. Stirrup to stirrup they set a brisk pace, pausing to rest the horses at intervals. Longstreet occupied the time with his own thoughts. Toward midday they drew a halt in a stand of cotton-woods grown up on the banks of a creek. They stepped down to water the horses and take a bite of hardtack in the shade. A cool breeze swirled off the front range, rippling the creek surface in golden light.

"You're mighty quiet. Not that it's any of my business, but somethin' eatin' at you?"

"Yeah, Maddie. She hasn't gotten over her abduction."

"Such things take time."

"I hope that's all it takes."

"You sound doubtful."

"I am."

"Now you sound concerned."

"I am that too. See, I asked her to marry me."

"Well, I'll be. That don't sound like a cause for concern."

"She said she needed to think it over. She's frightened for the work I do."

"There's other lines of work."

"I offered. She said she wouldn't ask that of me."

"Good women mostly don't. They take us pretty much the way we come, the bad with the good. I should know. Ain't never had one take me for what I am. At least not in a matrimonial way."

"Don't have any experience that way either. Never thought I'd feel that way toward one woman. Then I wake up one morning to find out I do and what happens? She won't have me."

"I didn't hear you say she said that. She said she needed to think it over."

"Yeah, I know. It doesn't feel like that though."

"If it's meant to be, it will be. These things go bad when what ain't meant to be is made to be. Come on, Pueblo's a waitin'."

Pueblo

The roundhouse presented a cavernous space constructed of stone and heavy timber on a siding north of the main line. Bat ordered the Gatling gun deployed facing the depot and town. Its field of fire commanded the yard leading to her main entrance. He positioned his men to perimeter and rear-guard stations. He stood at the front entrance beside the gun with Thompson, Short, Holliday, and Rudabaugh.

"Anybody ever fire one of these?" Bat asked.

No one offered.

"I made ice cream. I can learn," Rudabaugh said.

"I expect you can," Bat said.

"Point the thing and turn the crank. Next thing you know you're a whole damn army."

"Until you run out of rounds," Holliday said.

Short spoke up. "I'll feed the thing."

"Looks like we have a gun crew," Bat said. He followed a staircase with his eyes into the dark vault of the ceiling. A catwalk ran in a rectangle over the track used by crewmen servicing a locomotive. Light filtered through shutters to a window in a loft over the front door.

"See there, Doc?" He pointed to the catwalk and window. Holliday nodded.

"How about you take a watch on the town from up there. We'll relieve you in a couple of hours."

Doc disappeared in the shadows leading to the stairway.

"Now what?" Thompson asked.

"We wait."

Cane and Longstreet loped into town as the sun drifted toward the western horizon. They tied up at the sheriff's office. Sheriff Henley Price sat at his desk. Steel gray matched the sheriff's hair and eyes to features chiseled out of burnished rock. A string bow tie and gray flannel shirt left a slight paunch to his gun belt, but not a weakness a man cared to make too much of.

"Sheriff Price? Briscoe Cane, Great Western Detective League." Cane held out his hand to Price's firm grip. "My partner, Beau Longstreet."

Price and Longstreet exchanged greetings.

"I've been expecting you since I got the Colonel's wire."

"What are we up against?" Longstreet asked.

"Plenty. Let's take a walk."

They left the office and followed the sheriff west along the boardwalk into the slanting sun. The sheriff paused at the west end of town and lifted his mustache down the track. A massive building straddled a siding north of the main line.

"That there's the roundhouse. It's the key to controlling this end of the line."

"AT&S men have it?" Cane asked.

"Do they ever. Bat Masterson himself and some twelve to fourteen tough guns are in that building. If that weren't bad enough, see the crack in those double doors. You can't see it for the shadows now, but they've mounted a Gatling gun in there."

"Seems like they've taken a serious interest in holding the

place," Cane said.

"You might say."

"Briscoe here is a pretty fair hand with dynamite," Longstreet said. "A handcart with a load should do the trick."

"That'd take care of them, but it wouldn't do the Denver & Rio Grande much good. Like I said, you need that roundhouse to run the railroad. No, sir. We need a different way to crack that nut."

Cane stroked the stubble on his chin. "No trouble. We let 'em surrender."

"Bat Masterson and that crew. Surrender?" Price looked to Longstreet as if to say, someone here needs to talk sense.

"What are you thinkin', Briscoe?" Longstreet asked.

"We need a little help from the Colonel. Where's the Western Union office?"

Denver

League members and their posses fanned out along the right-of-way to the Royal Gorge. Station by station they served notice on Masterson's men occupying the disputed facilities. Little resistance was offered in the face of a definitive court order. One by one the reports arrived at League headquarters, notifying the Colonel this station or that depot was secure. Palmer marked off the reports on a route map. In a matter of days, it came down to the roundhouse.

"That about does it, Colonel. All we need now is the roundhouse."

"That lays the table the way Cane wants it."

"I'm not sure I follow."

"Briscoe Cane, one of my best operatives, is in Pueblo. Masterson himself is forted up there with his top gunnies and a Gatling gun."

"The roundhouse would make one hell of a fort. That said,

we need it in one piece. If it's damaged, we're going nowhere until it's repaired."

"Briscoe knows that. That's why they've made no attempt to evict Masterson and his men. Briscoe wanted it to come down to this. The dispute is over. The only thing left is to surrender the roundhouse. The law is with us. Masterson is a lawman. Briscoe believes he will accept that."

"I hope he's right. Masterson has a reputation too. He's not known for giving up."

"I'll wire Briscoe. We'll know soon enough."

Topeka

The note read: *Further instruction. Locomotive barn. Midnight.* It was signed simply *E.* Atkins scowled. What further instruction could you possibly need on a contract for murder? As long as this has taken and considering disposition of the litigation, his instruction might be *cancel the contract and give me my money back.* He dismissed that option. Chorus was meddlesome in more ways than one. Moreover, he doubted Esteban's associates dealt in refunds. The locomotive barn at midnight. Hell of a place for a meeting, unless . . .

He opened his right-hand desk drawer and drew out a .38 Colt pocket pistol. He spun the cylinder, checking the loads. He doubted the meeting put him in danger. The remainder of the contract represented a substantial sum. With no mention of that payment being due, he considered that sum an insurance policy. Still, one could never be too careful.

Midnight

The locomotive barn cast a long shadow against a moonlit night sky. Stars sparkled jewel-like on a black velvet drape. Atkins hauled lines and stepped down from his carriage. He lowered the tie-down and fastened the strap to the bay's bridle. He entered the barn through the front door to the street. Parallel tracks served the locomotives housed in the barn for maintenance. Cool air mingled with scents of steel, oil, coal, and grease. Engines parked in their places, slumbering black giants, starred here and there by pinpoints of brass light. The barn opened at both ends to ribbons of track silvered in moonlight. Atkins allowed his eyes to adjust. The Spaniard stood framed in silhouette by the lighted arch of the north engine yard.

Atkins's footfalls echoed in the cavern as he trudged to the north end of the barn. He adjusted the pistol in his trouser waistband from the cover of darkness before stepping into ambient light. Esteban stood unmoved, awaiting his approach.

"Further instructions? Why isn't the son of a bitch dead?"

"We encountered complications."

"Complications. Your friends are being paid handsomely to get a job done. That includes overcoming complications."

"Law enforcement happened on the scene at an inopportune time. Our man was killed. Other arrangements needed to be made."

"Regrettable. Why are you now in need of further instructions?"

"These complications have increased our cost."

"You want more money for a job your friends failed to accomplish?"

"Twenty thousand."

Atkins laughed. "You must be joking. Twice the price for a job you bungled? Chorus was a problem when the Royal Gorge right-of-way was at stake. In case you hadn't noticed, it no longer is. Now, if you'll return my initial payment, we'll simply forget this whole mishandled arrangement."

"I doubt that will be possible. My friend's contractual terms are . . . shall we say, final."

"In that case, there are no further instructions." Atkins turned to go.

The Spaniard sprang like a cat; covering Atkins's mouth with an iron grasp he jerked the railroad man's head back, exposing his throat to the blade. A rush of air burbled gouts of blood. The man's eyes shot round, white and dead. The body sank limp to the rough roadbed.

CHAPTER THIRTY-SIX

Pueblo

The telegram found Cane and Longstreet with Sheriff Price in his office as late afternoon sun waned in the west.

"Show's about over." Cane handed the telegram to Longstreet.

"What do you plan to do now?" Longstreet passed the foolscap to Price.

"Have a talk with Masterson."

"You think he'll listen?"

"Let's hope so. I don't fancy facing that gun. Sheriff, you got something that'll pass for a flag of truce?"

"I s'pect we got an old bedsheet for the jail we could rip up."

"That should work. Let's see if we can get this over before nightfall."

Ten minutes later Cane, Longstreet, and Price paused at the west end of town.

"You two stay here," Cane said.

"Someone's comin'," the lookout called from the catwalk. "Looks like he wants to parlay."

Rudabaugh scrambled to the gun and racked a round into the breech. Masterson and Thompson stood in the doorway.

"Just one," Thompson said. "Looks peaceful enough."

"Briscoe Cane," Masterson said.

"You know him?"

"By reputation."

"Competent?"

"With a gun, sure. Even better with a knife. That doesn't bother me."

"What does?"

"His other specialty."

"What's that?"

"Dynamite."

"Masterson, Briscoe Cane. We need to talk."

"I hear you."

"No need to shout half across town. Come on out where I can see you."

"Cover me, Ben. Dave, you keep that lead grinder out of this until I'm not in the line of fire. Got it?"

"Got it."

Masterson stepped through the doors and walked out to meet Cane.

"What's on your mind, Briscoe?"

"Show's over, Bat. Court decided for the Denver & Rio Grande. Great Western Detective League officers have secured the D&RG right-of-way. Everything except this here round-house. As a federal officer I'm sure you'll respect the court's decision."

"And if I don't?"

"That'd be most unfortunate."

"We got some tough guns in there along with that big one."

"I'm aware of that. We've got a handcart."

Masterson laughed. "A handcart?"

"With a fuse."

Silence.

"Good thing for old Palmer," Bat said.

"Good thing?"

"The court. Palmer got himself a roundhouse."

Denver

Headlines in the morning paper screamed:

Railroad Magnet Murdered

Crook took his morning coffee to his office and read.

Prominent Topeka railroad owner Stephen Atkins was found dead Monday morning in the Atkins, Topeka & Southern locomotive barn. Early arriving workers discovered the body. Mr. Atkins's throat had been cut . . .

The article continued on for several paragraphs discussing Atkins's many civic contributions to the community along with his business achievements. It went on to describe his involvement in the recent dispute over the Royal Gorge right-of-way to Leadville and the court settling the dispute in favor of the rival Denver & Rio Grande. No motive or suspects had yet been identified according to Sheriff Anderson Prescott. A line toward the end of the story brought Crook up full stop.

. . . curiously the third finger of the victim's left hand was missing.

Pueblo

The Colonel's telegram arrived as Longstreet and Cane were preparing to head back to Denver. Cane read the line.

"Third finger of the victim's left hand was missing."

"Ring finger," Longstreet said.

"El Anillo," Cane murmured.

"Looks like our snake has grown a new head."

"And we're bound for Topeka. We best stable these horses."

The eastbound rolled out at noon. Longstreet and Cane

entrained with Masterson and his men. Bat took a seat across the aisle from Cane. With the roundhouse hostilities settled Masterson gave way to curiosity.

"I can't believe we haven't crossed paths before this, Briscoe."

"We nearly did over the Sam Bass pursuit, as I recall the stories I heard."

"Not near enough. I got a long ride in rough country. You got Bass."

"A year later. We had our share of long rides in rough country before we caught up with him."

"So, tell me, is all that stuff I hear about you true?"

"What stuff?"

"The knives, the Henry rifle, dynamite, never mind those sidearms of yours."

"Oh, I don't know, you know how reputations go. What you hear is probably overblown."

"It's true," Longstreet said from the window seat.

Cane gave him a reproving headshake.

"I thought so," Bat said. "So, where you headed? I figured you'd be on your way back to Denver."

"We've got a case cropped up in Topeka."

"What kind of case?"

"Stephen Atkins's murder."

"What? Atkins murdered? When?"

"Couple days ago, while we were staring at each other over the roundhouse."

"Atkins hired me to raise a posse and secure his right-of-way holdings. What happened?"

"We don't know much. He was found in the locomotive barn with his throat cut."

"Any idea who did it?"

"Not exactly, but we have a pretty good idea who's behind it. Ever heard of El Anillo?"

"What's that?"

"Some real bad guys. El Anillo means 'ring.' Very silent. Very deadly. We thought we might have put them out of business when we killed the man who headed it up. Looks like the snake may have grown a new head."

"What makes you think it was them?"

"Trademark kill. Cut off the third finger of his left hand."

"The ring finger."

"That's it. The more interesting question is why? Why El Anillo? There seem to be two possibilities. Either Atkins and the ring were engaged in some criminal enterprise that went bad, or it was murder for hire."

"I knew Stephen Atkins. He's no criminal. Ruthless business-man, but criminal? I don't see it."

"If you're right, that leaves us another tough question. Who'd want him dead bad enough to buy an El Anillo assassination?"

CHAPTER THIRTY-SEVEN

Topeka

Longstreet and Cane stepped off the eastbound AT&S, to a hot gusty wind and blazing sunshine. They headed straight to Sheriff Anderson Prescott's office. They found the burly bear of a man with drooping mustaches and bushy sideburns at his desk. He glanced at his visitors.

"Sheriff, Briscoe Cane, Great Western Detective League. My partner, Beau Longstreet." Hands shook all around.

"I expected the Colonel would be sending someone. Atkins was a big man in these parts. Odd about that missing finger too."

"We've seen it before," Cane said. "Signature of a crime syndicate. Calls itself El Anillo."

"The ring."

"Ever heard of it?"

"Only whispers. Anybody who knows anything about it, keeps to themselves."

"For good reason," Longstreet said. "Any leads?"

Prescott scowled with a headshake. "Foreman found the body near dawn. Didn't see any sign of anyone on or about the premises."

"Not surprising. These people are professional. We thought we got the head of the outfit not long ago. It appears it didn't put them out of business."

"Did Atkins have any personal problems or enemies who

200

might have wanted him dead?" Cane asked.

"Not that I know of. Like I said, he was a pillar of the community."

"What becomes of the railroad?" Longstreet asked.

"Board named W. B. Strong acting president."

"Where can we find Mr. Strong? Maybe he can shed some light on this."

"I expect he's at the AT&S offices. I'll take you there."

The desk didn't feel comfortable. He glanced around not for the first time. The imposing desk, polished wood paneling, shelves lined in leather-bound books. Strong understood the job. He probably knew more about running a railroad than Atkins ever did. It wasn't tracklaying, roadbed maintenance, or locomotive repair that bothered him. He could handle those in his sleep. No, it was the unfamiliar duties. The board of directors, stockholders, bankers, lawyers, and such like that. He was a simple get-things-done guy. The subtleties of this office were what felt uncomfortable.

A rap at the door intruded on his reflections. Now what? That was the other thing about this office. Somebody always needed something.

"Sheriff Prescott and two gentlemen to see you, sir."

"Show them in."

Prescott led the way.

"Sheriff," Strong rose in greeting.

"Mr. Strong. Allow me to present Briscoe Cane and Beau Longstreet of the Great Western Detective League."

"Gentlemen," Strong said. "Have a seat. Has there been some development in the case?"

"Not so far. My office is a member of the League these gentlemen represent. They have some familiarity with the circumstances of the case. I'll let them explain."

"Before we begin," Longstreet said. "Just for the record, would you mind telling us where you were at the time of the murder?"

Strong darkened. "Surely you don't think that I . . ."

"I have to ask for the record."

"I was near end of track in Pueblo. The crew there can attest to that."

"Thank you. We believe the organization responsible for Mr. Atkins's murder is a crime syndicate known as El Anillo."

"A crime syndicate, what makes you think that?"

"The deceased's ring finger. It is a signature for one of their killings."

"Yes, that was curious."

"El Anillo leads to two possibilities," Cane said. "Is it possible Mr. Atkins was involved in some dealing with them that went bad?"

"Stephen? A crime syndicate? Surely you jest."

"I assure you, Mr. Strong, the question is no jest."

"I can't imagine such a thing. Stephen was a pillar of the community. The emblem of integrity."

"So we are told."

"There must be some other explanation."

Longstreet fixed on Strong's reaction to Briscoe's next question.

"The other possibility is murder for hire. Someone wanted Mr. Atkins dead bad enough to pay El Anillo to kill him."

Strong furrowed his brow, absorbing the information.

"Did Mr. Atkins have that kind of enemy, Mr. Strong?"

"I can't think that he did, can you, Sheriff?"

Prescott shook his head.

"Unless . . ." Strong trailed off.

"Unless what, Mr. Strong?"

"The Royal Gorge right-of-way dispute was certainly contentious. It's possible it could have given rise to that kind of animosity."

"You're suggesting someone with a stake in the Denver & Rio Grande might have had motive," Longstreet said.

"It's possible."

"But the suit was settled in their favor before the murder."

Cane smoothed his mustache between thumb and forefinger. "The outcome may have been in doubt at the time the contract was made."

"That too is possible," Longstreet said. "Then who might have had such a stake?"

"Palmer," Strong said.

CHAPTER THIRTY-EIGHT

Denver

Crook drummed his fingers on the desk, the telegram from Longstreet tossed aside in the wake of his reading. He didn't like it. Gray light and the patter of rain on the roof matched his mood. Palmer a murder suspect? Like it or not, circumstantial logic leaned in that direction. The question begged. *What is to be done about it?*

The very idea of broaching the subject didn't sit well. Palmer was a client, a respected member of the community. Discomfort or no, something needed to be done. Nothing difficult ever came easily. He needed a second opinion, but whose? An unlikely ally might serve. He rose from his desk, collected his umbrella, and left the office for the short walk to the Denver offices of the Pinkerton Agency.

The rain spatter on his umbrella did little to soften his mood. He presented himself at the Pinkerton office. Presently he was admitted to the office of a somewhat surprised Reginald Kingsley.

"Colonel Crook, I must say how unexpected."

"I'm sure it is, Reggie."

"To what do I owe so dubious a distinction?"

"Professional courtesy."

"Now there's a first. How may I assist?"

"I need a professional opinion."

"I'm listening."

"You're aware, I presume, of Stephen Atkins's murder."

"Pity that. Quite a good customer. Always paid promptly."

"Yes, well pleased as I am to hear that, I've come into some rather disturbing information in the course of our investigation. I'd be interested in your estimation of it."

Kingsley made a steeple of his fingertips and tilted his head, attentive.

"Atkins's murder has the mark of El Anillo about it."

"The ring finger. I recall thinking as much as I read the newspaper account. Odd really, after your recent success in disposing of Don Victor."

"Precisely. We may have gotten the Don, but it appears the organization, or elements of it, survive. There can only be two explanations for the ring's involvement in Atkins's death."

"And they would be?"

"A deal gone bad, or murder for hire."

"Seems reasonable."

"It seems we can rule out a deal gone bad for the moment. Atkins, it appears, was the paragon of integrity."

"Wouldn't be the first time the lofty have fallen."

"True, but bear with me. Absent any obvious indications of impropriety, we are left with the murder for hire possibility. That begs the question, who might have wanted Atkins dead sufficiently to have hired El Anillo to do it? Again, the man himself appears to have had few enemies."

"To my point of a lofty fall."

"Circumstance suggests there may be one rival with motive." Kingsley's eyes rounded. "You're not thinking . . ."

"Thinking what?"

"Palmer?"

"Who else?"

"I make it a bridge too far."

"Why?"

Kingsley smoothed his mustache in thought. "I believe I see your dilemma. Still Palmer secured his victory in court. He had no need to eliminate Atkins."

"That was a more recent development. What might Palmer have thought with the dispute still in doubt?"

"I don't relish that line of reasoning."

"Neither do I, but what's to be done about it?"

"Capture the El Anillo operative and ferret out the truth."

"Sad as the admission may be on both of our accounts, our record in such pursuits is something less than sterling."

Kingsley pursed his lips as though chewing a sour pickle. "I suppose you've a point there."

"The only avenue I see is to confront Palmer with the possibility and judge his response. He's no hardened criminal. Between us, we may have the judgment to assess his character. It's no assurance, but it seems a stone best overturned."

"So, it's my judgment you value. Extraordinary really. But I'm afraid, your show. Your stone."

"So you won't assist me?"

"Palmer too has been a good client. I've already lost one. What have I to gain for risking alienation of another?"

"Is that all it is to you, Reggie? Business? What of justice?"

"Justice is blindfolded for a reason."

"Yes, I've observed that by some of your tactics. Perhaps in coming here I overestimated your preference for proper outcome." Crook rose to take leave.

"Oh, all right, Colonel. I shall accompany you if I must. I'm not thoroughly jaded, you know. Merely appreciative of opportunity is all."

Palmer read the weekly progress report on Royal Gorge construction to the accompaniment of raindrops splattering the office windowpane. He noted questions in the margin he would wire the chief engineer for clarification. They'd paid up the wages on trestle work to a level that should keep the Knights of Labor at bay. It was expensive, but not so when compared to the cost of a strike, as AT&S found out. He pushed impatience aside. Soon enough they'd open the road to lucrative silver shipments from Leadville.

"Colonel Crook and Mr. Kingsley to see you, sir."

He glanced at the office door. Crook and Kingsley? Had he heard right? Odd.

"Send them in, Vincent."

Crook led the way.

Palmer smiled. "Gentlemen, I must say I never expected such . . . an auspicious delegation."

"Neither did we," Kingsley said.

"Please have seats. To what do I owe the pleasure?"

Sir Reggie deferred to Crook.

"We've come in regard to the Atkins murder case."

Palmer shook his head. "Tragic that. Stephen and I had our differences, but who could wish such a fate on anyone? Barbaric really, I do hope you bring the perpetrator to justice."

"The very question we've come to discuss."

"I'm afraid I don't understand."

"Does the name El Anillo mean anything to you?"

Palmer furrowed his brow quizzically. "Can't say that it does. Should it?"

"We believe El Anillo is responsible for Atkins's death."

"I don't see the connection."

"Among other things, they do murder for hire."

White swelled in Palmer's eyes. "Someone paid to have Stephen killed?"

"It appears so."

"But who? Who would do such a thing?"

"Someone with motive."

"Motive? I doubt Stephen had many enemies."

"Even you?"

"Me? We had a business rivalry. We settled it in court like civilized businessmen."

"How do you contact them?"

"Contact who?"

"El Anillo."

"I told you, I have no idea who you are talking about. I'm beginning to resent this line of questioning, Colonel. Do you have a specific allegation to make?"

Crook looked at Kingsley.

"I'm back to the lofty fallen."

Crook nodded agreement.

"No, William. We had a lead to follow. I'm sorry for the implication."

Palmer mopped a sheen of sweat from his brow with a handkerchief. "I've never been accused of murder before. I can't say I care to ever have the experience again."

CHAPTER THIRTY-NINE

O'Rourke House
Denver
1910

I put my pencil down on the pad in my lap. "That didn't really happen, did it?"

Cane looked at me with a half-smile. "What, you don't believe me?"

"The Colonel turned to Kingsley for assistance. I don't believe it."

"Believe it."

"I can't imagine him admitting such a thing."

"Were he still telling the story, you might never have heard it."

"But why would he do such a thing?"

"Omit that detail?"

"No, no. I can well imagine that. Why would he have turned to Sir Reggie?"

"One thing you must know about the Colonel above all else."

"What's that?"

"He would solve a case, no stone left unturned. Reggie was a rascal, not to be trusted to be sure. That said, he was also a good investigator. For all the Colonel's dislike for the man, he respected his investigative skill."

"And Kingsley? Would he have turned to the Colonel under similar circumstances?"

"I'll wager not."

"You mean he didn't respect the Colonel?"

"Oh, I'm sure he did. Properly so too."

"Then why wouldn't he have consulted the Colonel?"

"Pride. Reggie could never admit to needing anyone's help."

"Even if he did?"

"Even if he did. That's what made the Colonel a better investigator than his lordship."

"What an odd relationship."

"Competition often forges unlikely alliances."

"So where then did the investigation next proceed?"

Cane drifted off. "Longstreet came onto a hunch. A good one too, apart from a painful consequence."

Topeka

Longstreet and Cane checked into their hotel and headed for the saloon. They grabbed a quiet table and signaled the bartender for a bottle and two glasses. Cane dropped two dollars on the table. The bartender poured and left the bottle.

Longstreet studied his glass in thought.

"I can all but hear the wheels grind in that head of yours," Cane said. "What are you chewing on?"

"Call it a hunch."

"All right. What hunch are you chewin' on?"

"The Spaniard."

"Why him?"

"We know he was with the Don at Chorus's place. According to Maddie he left in a hurry to go someplace."

"Right about the time we got the tip from Henley Price."

"Yup. In Pueblo."

"Not far from Manitou Springs."

"No, it's not far and Pueblo has AT&S service to Topeka."

"Interesting." Cane tossed off his drink and poured another.

"It's a possibility. How do you suppose Henley got his tip?"

"Search me."

"Maybe we best find out. I'll wire him in the morning."

Cane took a bright sunlit table in the hotel dining room. He ordered bacon, eggs, biscuits, and coffee. Longstreet arrived on the heels of the waiter with a telegram in one hand. He passed it to Cane. Cane read. Longstreet ordered breakfast.

"Telegram tip from Topeka. Seems like we got us a suspect."

"It does," Longstreet said. "How'd he get Atkins into a locomotive barn in the dark of night?"

"Good question. Maybe Atkins wasn't as lily white as his reputation suggests."

"He must have had some reason for being there."

"So, if the Spaniard is our man, where do you suppose he is now?"

"Another good question. If I were a betting man . . ."

"You're the one with the hunches."

"I'd bet on El Paso."

"You think he's the Don's next in line?"

"You have a better idea?"

"Let the Colonel make that call."

"I'll wire him after breakfast."

That evening Crook ordered Longstreet and Cane to El Paso by return wire.

Cañon City

Early morning filtered sepia through lace curtains, casting the spare room a glow. Samantha watched the light play over the planes of Trevor's chest in the rise and fall of his breathing. She enjoyed the idle aftermath of the assignment. Trevor proved as ever a delightful amusement, though the familiar tug of restlessness told her soon enough it would be time to move on.

His eyelids fluttered. One cracked open to her. "See anything that interests you?"

She smiled, playfully lifting the sheet. "Perhaps."

He turned to her, propped on an elbow. His gaze wondered over the swell of her hip.

"Now what," he said.

"Now what, indeed."

"No, there." He lifted his chin to the door.

She rolled to her back. A small yellow envelope lay on the floor. "Kingsley, I'll wager." She rolled out of bed to the complaint of the springs and fetched the telegram. She felt his eyes follow her.

"It's for you." She handed him the envelope and climbed back in bed.

He tore it open and read. "Party's over. I'm to return to Denver."

"I suppose that means I should return to Chicago."

"Must you?"

"Dear boy," she traced his cheek with a finger. "It's been lovely, but as they say 'All good things . . .' "

He pulled her to his kiss.

". . . 'come to an end.' Slowly."

Another kiss. Rhapsody in springs.

By way of Denver.

CHAPTER FORTY

Manitou Springs

A carriage crested the mesa and wound its way toward Chorus's estate hidden in blue shadow near sunset. Esteban wheeled his horse at the entry plaza and drew a halt. He climbed down and secured the tie-down. The heavy knocker sounded like a pistol shot in the stillness. Moments passed. The door swung open to Chorus himself.

"Señor Esteban, I wasn't sure I should see you again."

"We have a contract to fulfill. I have done so. Where is Don Victor?"

"Please come in." He closed the door behind his visitor. "I'm afraid I have some bad news. Your Don is dead."

"Dead? What happened?"

"They came for the woman."

"As expected."

"Not as expected. Longstreet did not come alone. The one they call Cane killed Don Victor."

"Where is Julio?"

Chorus shrugged. "He escaped."

Esteban absorbed the news.

"Come into the library," Chorus said. "You look as though you could use a drink."

Esteban followed his host, numbed at the news.

"Please, have a seat." Chorus busied himself at the sideboard, pouring two snifters of brandy. He carried them to the wing chairs beside the fireplace where the Spaniard had taken his seat. Esteban accepted the glass. "What does this mean to your El Anillo?"

Esteban looked perplexed. "The Don's death?"

Chorus nodded.

"It means Esteban is El Capitán," the assassin said.

"The ring continues then?"

"The ring is unbroken."

"And you say you have completed our contract."

"Sí."

"Then I shall pay the final agreed price."

"Bueno."

"What will you do now?"

"That is information it would be best if you did not have."

"I see. What about this Cane and Longstreet?"

"That is why it is best you do not know my plans. Time will provide opportunity to deal with them on our terms. For now, it is better they do not know the ring is unbroken."

"Then may I call on El Anillo in the future should the need arise?"

"Sí." Esteban drained his glass.

Chorus rose to refill it. "Then we should drink to the prospects of our continued association. You must stay the evening before you return."

El Paso

Sheriff Pablo Rojas sipped a cup of coffee gone strong in the pot over the course of a long morning. He leafed through a stack of dodgers on suspects wanted in the territory. The office door opened to a splash of midday sunlight. His black mustaches lifted in a grin of recognition and greeting.

"Longstreet, Cane." He rose. "Didn't expect to see you two again after I heard you took down Don Victor."

Cane took his hand. "We thought we might have seen the last of El Anillo too."

"No such luck it would appear," Longstreet said.

"Have seats. You're welcome to a cup of this coffee if you're partial to tarring your inwards."

"With a recommendation like that, I'll pass until bar time," Cane said.

"So, you're telling me our mysterious friends aren't as out of business as I thought."

"Doesn't seem so," Longstreet said. "Did you hear about Stephen Atkins's murder?"

"Saw something about it in the newspaper. Not much detail. Throat cut. Unknown assailant. No known motive. Not much to go on."

"Ring finger missing," Cane said.

Rojas sipped his coffee. "El Anillo signature. With the Don dead along with the ferret-faced killer, who did the work?"

"We don't exactly know. Beau here has a hunch."

Rojas glanced to Longstreet.

"The Don abducted the woman I hope to make my wife in revenge for my putting an end to Escobar, or the ferret as you call him. He was traveling with one of his goons and a more genteel sort we think is a Spaniard, goes by the name Esteban. The goon was with the Don when Briscoe and I came for Maddie. That's when the Don played his last hand. The goon got away. The Spaniard wasn't there. He'd left right around the time we got a tip on where the Don had taken Maddie. The tip placed the informant in Topeka in time for Atkins's murder."

"So, you figure your Spaniard for Atkins's killer."

"Sure feels like a prominent line of reason," Cane said.

"Which brings you two down here to see what you might find at the Don's hacienda."

"You know, Beau, if I didn't know better, I'd say Pablo here has a future in law enforcement."

"Careful. You get a collar in my jurisdiction, you'll need a warrant. I'd be nice to me if I were you."

They all laughed.

"Come on. Let's rent you two a couple of horses. We'll ride out there in the morning."

They rode into the hill country on a bright morning just after dawn. The trail climbed into the narrow defile, winding its way up and around to the blind side of a hill. Cane noticed what appeared to be recent horse droppings. Someone had been through here within the past few days. Rojas drew rein at the crest of a ridge, leading onto a plateau. The low, rambling El Anillo hacienda could be seen across an expanse of no more than a quarter mile where it blended into a sheer rock wall climbing behind it. There appeared no sign of life.

"How do you want to play this?" Rojas asked.

Longstreet cut his eyes to Cane.

Cane shrugged. "I'll ride on in and knock at the door. Beau, you swing in wide from the right. Sheriff, you do the same on the left. That way we've got some cover for each other." Cane led them out. He took an easy trot across the plateau, approaching the plaza fronting the hacienda. Still no sign of life. He drew rein and stepped down. Morning breeze swirled dust across the stone plaza leading to the front entrance. Cane ran his gaze over the windows. Dark and quiet. The roof line too showed no sign of movement. He approached the heavy wooden door and gave it a rap. Nothing. He tried the door. It opened to a dark foyer within. He listened.

"Yo, the house."

No answer. He waved Longstreet and Rojas in. Moments later they stepped down.

"Sheriff, check around the back. Beau, cover me. I'm going in."

Rojas drifted off skirting the hacienda to the north and west. Cane drew his .44, Longstreet his Lightning. Cane stepped into the foyer and paused, letting his eyes adjust to the dim window light. A large, comfortably furnished parlor sprawled away to the right. Two corridors led away from the foyer, one to the back of the house, the other to the left.

"Keep an eye out, Beau." He took the corridor on the left. Wooden doors lined both sides, recessed in thick adobe walls. The first door on the left opened with a complaint on its hinges. The room admitted light to the corridor. The sleeping chamber contained a bed, table, chair, and wardrobe. The next door on the right opened to a windowless sleeping chamber that gave no light. Cane claimed a bedside lamp from the first bedroom, scratched a match, and trimmed it to light. The corridor search yielded four more similarly empty rooms. Cane returned to the foyer.

"Anything?" Longstreet asked.

"Nothing." Cane turned to the back of the house. The corridor led to a spacious study behind the parlor on the right. To the left, a dining room with a long formal table, seating twelve. Cane crossed the dining room, aware of Longstreet following him down the corridor. At the far end of the room a service door led to a large kitchen. He glanced around the room. His eye came to rest on the stove. He opened the grate. Ashes radiated a hint of warmth. Someone was here and not that long ago. He returned to find Longstreet in the dining room.

"Ashes in the stove are still warm."

"Someone's been here."

"Let's see what Rojas found."

Back outside they rounded to the back of the hacienda where they found a stable, a corral, and the sheriff with a man dressed in the loose-fitting blouse and pantaloons of a peon.

"What have we here?" Cane asked.

"Local, Ramon is his name. He looks after the place. What did you find?"

"Nothing. Nobody here, though the stove ashes are still warm. What does he know?"

"Not much. He's mute. He signed his Patrón is gone."

"Well, we know one won't be coming back. Is it possible a new Patrón has moved in?" Longstreet said.

"Like I said, he's mute. So what do we do now?"

"We ride out," Cane said.

They watched the riders cross the plateau from the mouth of a cave high up in the rock wall behind the hacienda.

"What do you make of it?" Julio asked.

Esteban narrowed his eyes in thought. "They did not find us, did they?"

"No."

"Es Bueno. We may have to lay low a few days, but with nothing to see they will soon go away. Come, let us go back down to the hacienda where we can be more comfortable. El Anillo is unbroken. This is most important."

El Capitán led the way to the back of the cave. He struck a match to a lamp and trimmed the wick. A stairway cut into a tunnel passage led down through the hillside to a wardrobe in the furthest back bedroom.

CHAPTER FORTY-ONE

Denver

Crook listened, fingers tented to his lips haloed in lamplight. Cane and Longstreet dragged in just in time to catch him before he closed up to end the day. The story lacked the closure they might have hoped for.

"So, you found no sign of this Esteban and no one at the hacienda other than the mute."

"That's about it," Longstreet said.

"What do you make of it?"

"The Atkins's killing was an El Anillo job," Cane said. "Esteban was in Topeka. Either he did the work or had it done. Either way, he's our man for now. If you rule out Palmer, it's anybody's guess what the motive might have been. What makes you and Sir Reggie so sure it wasn't Palmer?"

"Palmer had already won the Royal Gorge dispute. He was actually saddened at the news of Atkins's death. They were strong-willed competitors, but that stops well short of murder. He made no recognition of El Anillo when confronted with the name."

"Accomplished liars have feigned sorrow and ignorance before."

"Precisely why I broke down and took Reggie along. I wanted a second opinion. He may be a scoundrel, but he is an effective investigator."

Crook drummed his fingers on the desk. "Now this comes in

219

the category of pure speculation, but we know where Esteban was when he left for Topeka."

"Chorus," Cane said. "But the Don and his men were there to kill him."

"They were, but they didn't kill him, did they? Assassins get paid to kill people. Do they care who they kill? Or do they care more about being paid?"

"Are you suggesting Chorus bought off Don Victor and turned El Anillo to murder Atkins?" Longstreet asked.

"I'm suggesting the possibility. The Don used Chorus's estate to lure you into a trap with Maddie. If it were you, and you had a contract to kill the old recluse, why would you keep him, how did he phrase it?"

"A prisoner in his own home."

"Exactly. Why would you do that? You'd kill him first and then lay your trap. I doubt he was a prisoner at all. He merely used captivity as a convenient ruse to explain why he was still alive."

"Let's assume Chorus did buy his own life. Why would Chorus want Atkins killed?" Longstreet asked.

"Still leaves us short on a motive. If I had to guess, I'd say it has something to do with the Royal Gorge. It could be all that lovely silver or something to do with the right-of-way dispute."

"Speculation aside," Cane said, "if he didn't return to El Paso, the Spaniard could be anywhere."

"Sheriff Rojas promised to check on the hacienda from time to time to see if anyone showed up there," Longstreet said. "Past that, all we have to go on is the usual."

"Put out the word to the League and be on the lookout for his next move," Crook said.

The moon rose full, climbing over the treetops as Longstreet hurried up the street to O'Rourke House. *Maddie.* She'd occupied his thoughts all the long way back to Denver. *How would he find her? Might she have reached a decision? Who could say?* He'd know soon enough, swinging through the front gate to a familiar welcoming groan.

The door swung open to familiar scents of fresh baked bread and floor polish. "It's the bad penny. He's turned up again."

Mrs. Fitzwalter poked her head out of the kitchen. She wiped her hand on her apron. In the kitchen. What was she doing there?

"Beau," she said. Her eyes clouded sober.

"Where's Maddie?"

"She's . . . she's gone."

"Gone? When will she be back?"

"She left this for you." She took an envelope from the sideboard, handed it to him, and returned to the kitchen as if unsure what more to do.

He tore it open.

My Dearest Beau,

It is with heartfelt pain and sorrow that I put pen to this paper. I cannot bear the thought of losing you for a decision I cannot escape. For all that I love you, and I do, I cannot be your wife. The thought of what you do and the risks you take would haunt my every waking hour for whatever life we might have together. I know you have said you would give it up and find some other pursuit, but I cannot persuade myself such would be fair to you. I love the man you are and I shall cling to that memory. I shall not change it. These weeks in your absence have accorded me time for clear-headed thinking. I've been widowed for some time now. It's not the end of the world, but I shouldn't wish to endure such loss again. I know life comes with risk. In this, my love, I'll not tempt the fates.

I've sold the house to Mrs. Fitzwalter at a fair price with her assurance you are welcome to continue living there. Proceeds of the sale will allow me to reestablish myself and resume those rules that served me so well for so long. You did make a mockery of them and I shall love you forever for it.

Maddie

The letter dropped to his side, clutched in trembling fingers. His gut turned a knot. He stepped to the kitchen door. Mrs. Fitzwalter turned from the stove.

"Where did she go?"

"She knew you would ask. She didn't say. I'm sorry, Beau. I know how hard this must be for you. She agonized over it I can tell you. In the end, Maddie O'Rourke is who she is. I believe she prized you for who you are."

"I'm not sure what to make of that me at this moment. I'm going for a walk. Please don't wait supper for me."

O'Rourke House
1910

I glanced across the parlor to the very dining room where Longstreet read her letter. Visions of my own impending nuptials swirled through my head. Cane cleared his throat.

"Didn't see that coming, did you?"

"No, I certainly did not. I can imagine how I would feel if such were to befall my Penny and me."

"Hard for a time as she knew it would be. She also knew Beau for a tough resilient fellow who'd come back to himself in time."

"I suppose so. It's only that it's so abrupt. Marriage proposals one minute, gone in the next."

"For now."

"For now? Then you know what became of her?"

"I said it's a long story. Best we don't get ahead of ourselves."

I furrowed a brow, sensed I was being played. "In some ways you're as bad as the Colonel."

"Why, thank you. Those are impressive shoes to be likened in."

"Taken as wished, never mind the intention."

"A privilege of age. One day you'll likely earn the privilege too. For now, indulge me."

"All right. At least until next week."

Cane watched young Robert show himself out.

Angela emerged from the dining room carrying two cut crystal glasses.

"My turn."

"Your turn. Your turn for what?"

"Some of your story. Mother never told me how she acquired this house. I thought you might indulge me with it along with a touch of your weekly stipend."

Cane caught the mischievous sparkle in her eye as she held out the glasses. He poured.

"How much did you overhear?"

"Only the part about Maddie selling the house to Mother."

"Do you often listen in to our conversations?"

"The stories are interesting. Are they private?"

"Not hardly, but what possible interest could you have in hearing them?"

"Oh, I don't know, just curious, I suppose."

He handed her a glass and lifted his own. "Just curious?"

"Just curious."

"Curious about anyone in particular?" He touched the rim of her glass.

"Don't flatter yourself."

"I don't. You do."

She blushed a swallow. "Well, you won't tell me who you

were back then. The tales you tell young Robert will have to suffice. Now why did Maddie sell Mother the house?"

"You'd likely have to read the letter she left for Beau to figure that out. All we really know is that she declined his offer of marriage, sold her house to your mother, and departed."

"For parts unknown."

"At the time."

"Then there's more to the story."

"What's more to tell? Your mother owned this house and now you do, which as a tenant, I find a most agreeable arrangement."

"I'm sure you do. All the comforts of home and none of the domestic responsibilities."

"I help."

"After a fashion, not that that's the point. At least Longstreet managed the notion of a proposal."

"Overcame his ways he did and look what it got him, a broken heart."

"Broken heart. You'd have to have one to risk it." She drained her glass.

"I've risked it." He took her in his arms and kissed her sweetly.

"You are a risk," she said.

"You're not thinking of selling the house, are you?"

"Sell it? I don't even know why I own it."

CHAPTER FORTY-TWO

Denver

Cane arrived at the office the following morning to find Longstreet's desk unoccupied. He rapped lightly at the Colonel's door. He sat silhouetted in bright morning light streaming through his office window.

"Where's Beau?"

"I told him to take some time off."

"What do I have to do to get an assignment like that?"

"Find yourself a woman who'll turn down your marriage proposal and break your heart."

"Maddie?"

"None other."

"Beau's clever. They'll talk their way through it."

"Not likely. She's gone. Sold the house and left."

"For where?"

"Parts unknown."

"Why?"

"You'll have to ask Longstreet. I'm in criminal investigation. Lonely hearts are beyond me. While we're on the subject of criminal investigation, have a seat. I have a thought."

Cane took a chair.

"The Chorus question in Atkins's murder is stuck in my craw. I think we should have another chat with Mr. Palmer at the Denver & Rio Grande."

"But I thought you and Reggie ruled him out. What's he got

to do with Chorus?"

"Chorus is a financier. Could he have had a stake in the Royal Gorge dispute? A stake big enough to justify Atkins's demise."

"Seems like a leap, but I suppose it's possible."

"Come on, let's pay a call on Mr. Palmer."

D&RG Offices

"Colonel Crook and Mr. Cane to see you, sir."

Palmer looked up from the Royal Gorge progress report he'd been reading. *Crook? What could he want?* "Send them in, Vincent."

The assistant stepped aside and held the door, showing Crook and Cane into the office. He closed the door after them but did not return to his desk.

"Colonel, to what do I owe the unexpected pleasure?"

"William, this is my associate Briscoe Cane."

Palmer extended a hand. "Please have a seat."

"We're doing some follow-up on the Atkins murder case."

Palmer pulled a frown. "I thought we'd been all through that."

"We have as to your interest in the case. We're pursuing a different angle this time. Does the name Eli Chorus mean anything to you?"

Palmer straightened in surprise. "Why, yes, Mr. Chorus is one of our largest shareholders. You can't possibly think Eli had anything to do with Stephen's demise."

"It's only a suspicion. The ring responsible for Atkins's death also had a contract to kill Chorus."

"My heavens, they haven't killed Eli too, have they?"

"No, Mr. Chorus is alive and quite well. The ring used his estate to hold a hostage while attempting to entrap another of my operatives. The plot failed, resulting in the death of the ring's leader. The man we believe responsible for Atkins's murder left the estate bound for Topeka before my men rescued the hostage."

"And you think that implicates Eli in Atkins's death?"

"I think it's curious the ring didn't fulfill its contract to kill Chorus and suddenly turned on Atkins. Chorus's shareholdings in the Denver & Rio Grande gave him a stake in the Royal Gorge dispute. Is it possible he and Atkins may have had bad blood between them? Who might have engaged the ring to kill Chorus? Might it have been Atkins? Is it possible Chorus bought off the ring in exchange for returning the favor?"

"That's a lot of speculation, Colonel."

"It is. Sometimes speculation leads to the root of an investigation."

"Well, I'm afraid I can't shed much light on your thinking."

"You already have, William. You've told me Chorus may have had motive."

Manitou Springs

Muffled knocking at the front door stopped Chorus from crawling into bed. He checked his watch and read ten o'clock. *Who could be calling at this hour?* The knocking grew insistent. He drew a revolver from the nightstand and picked up the bedside lamp. Clad in his nightshirt, he padded down the hall and the stairway leading to the foyer. He paused at the door.

"Who is it?"

"Vincent, Mr. Chorus."

"Vincent," he unbolted the heavy door and opened it. "What are you doing here?"

"Something I overheard today. I thought you should know."

"Whatever couldn't wait for our usual communication?"

"I couldn't take the chance."

"Come in, come in." He led the way to the parlor. "Would

you care for a brandy?"

"Please."

Chorus poured two snifters from a cut-glass decanter and carried them to a side table between two wing chairs.

"Now, Vincent, pray tell what's so urgent?"

"Colonel Crook and a Mr. Cane of the Great Western Detective League called on Mr. Palmer today in regard to the matter of Stephen Atkins's murder."

Chorus knit his brows. "And how is that of concern to me?"

"Atkins was murdered by something Crook called a ring. He said they had a contract to kill you. The ringleader was found here when Crook's men freed a hostage. The man Crook believes killed Atkins was also here but left before Crook's men arrived. Crook inquired as to your holdings in D&RG stock. He said it establishes your stake in the Royal Gorge dispute. He speculates you may have bought off the ring for your own life and in turn paid them to kill Atkins."

Chorus turned the information over in his mind. "Speculation, it's all just wild speculation."

"I thought so, but I felt I should warn you as Crook or his operatives are likely to come calling."

"Likely so. And thanks to your diligence, Vincent, I shall be ready for them." He smiled over a sip of brandy. "Now you shall have to stay the night. Will you be missed at work tomorrow?"

"I left a note, claiming illness."

"Very clever. You shall return tomorrow with a handsome bonus to show for your effort. Now, may I freshen your glass?"

U.P. Hotel
Cheyenne

Maddie sat at the breakfast table pushing her eggs around a plate full of possibilities. Where to? The rails rattled east and west from here. Sacramento? San Francisco? Los Angeles? Nice enough though none spoke to her. East? She'd find Irish community in the East, though they tended to cluster in second-class neighborhoods for self-preservation. Short on opportunity for a woman to support herself decently. After all these years she had to admit she had the West in her blood. She needed to put Denver some distance behind her. For fear he might find her? More likely for fear she might find him. What to do?

She glanced at the newspaper folded on the table. A story caught her eye. It reported on the cattle business booming in the Wyoming basin. Large ranching interests were bringing untold wealth and prosperity to Cheyenne in the south, while small ranching interests were growing up in the north around places like Sheridan and Buffalo. She read. She knew nothing of the cattle business, but promising growth opportunities were always in need of one thing she possessed. Money. She had proceeds from the sale of O'Rourke House. Proceeds that would increase in value in a community coming into its own. Where is Buffalo, Wyoming? How does a person get there?

She scooped up the last of her elusive egg, dabbed her lips with a napkin, and pushed back from the table armed with new purpose.

O'Rourke House

Familiar surroundings turned quiet, hollow, empty. Longstreet found no escape in sleep. He stared into the still darkness absorbing his loss. Unknown finality left him powerless to do anything that might remedy his circumstances. Losing the war was painful. This loss was different, more personally painful. The cause they'd lost earned a loyalty wrenched away in defeat. This loss tore out a piece of him, leaving a bleeding wound impervious to staunch. *Why? Where could she have gone?* Surely they could have found a way short of this. She'd not given that possibility a chance. *Did she not care enough for him to try that?*

No, she cared for him sure enough. The answer lie in her leaving. No trace. She didn't trust herself. Alone she could wrap herself in the comforter of her rules, free of the risk he might again touch her heart. *Could he let her go?* It seemed he had no choice.

He'd not begin to heal, sitting here in the dark. The future stretched beyond the walls of this house. Time off? To what good purpose? Time to go back to work.

CHAPTER FORTY-THREE

The carriage rocked along, traversing wooded hills on the winding road to the Chorus estate. Dark rumpled clouds poured over the mountaintops, threatening a storm. Wind whipped dust from carriage wheels and horses' hooves. Cane drove while the Colonel mulled a line of questioning, circling the one stumbling block to his reasoning, proof. Poker players bluffed all the time. He needed a bluff to draw Chorus into self-incrimination.

"How do you plan to play this?" Cane asked as if reading his thoughts.

"Not sure. I been chewing that cabbage for the past few miles. All we've got is suspicion unless he gives himself up. We need a bluff that might squeeze him."

"What if we caught the goon they called Julio. He got away the night we rescued Maddie. Suppose he turned talkative. That might make him uncomfortable."

"It might, but you and I both know those El Anillo boys would as soon have their tongues cut out as betray the ring. Chances are if Chorus did employ them, he knows that too."

"So best keep it simple."

"All right, how?"

"The Atkins killing was El Anillo. The ring is still in business. Last we knew, they had a contract to kill him. We're concerned for his safety. See how he reacts."

"Good start. We can also ask if he overheard any talk about where the Spaniard went and what he was up to. The more we get him to talk, the better the chance he might trip himself up."

The road leveled out across the mesa top on the run up to the estate. Cane drew rein on the entrance drive. He stepped down and dropped the tie-down. He led Crook to the entrance and rapped the door knocker. The door opened to the imposing figure of a large black man whose white coat might have been stretched over chiseled granite. Bright black eyes, shining bald pate, and powerful shoulders tapered to a trim waist.

"Yes?" The word resonated chest deep.

"Is Mr. Chorus in?" Cane asked.

"Who may I say is calling?"

"Colonel David Crook and Briscoe Cane of the Great Western Detective League."

"A moment." The door closed. Footfalls died away beyond.

"Added security," Cane said.

"It would seem so."

The door opened. "This way, please."

He led the way down a polished wood corridor to the eccentric financier's library. Chorus awaited them clad in a dark red jacket.

"Mr. Cane," he extended a frail hand.

"Mr. Chorus, may I present Colonel David Crook, chief of our Great Western Detective League."

"Colonel, to what do I owe such a distinguished visit?"

"We're following the Stephen Atkins murder case."

"Ah yes, tragic news that. Please have seats." He led the way to velvet-covered chairs clustered around a table set before the fireplace. "May I offer you coffee or another libation?"

"Coffee," Crook said.

"Please," Cane added.

"Tobias." The black man disappeared. "Now what brings your investigation of poor Stephen's untimely passing to my door?"

"The murderer," Crook said to no particular reaction.

"The murderer? I'm afraid I don't understand."

"Atkins was murdered by an organization with which I believe you are familiar, El Anillo."

"The men who invaded my home." He looked to Cane for confirmation.

"The men who came to kill you," Cane said.

"For a mercy you and your Mr. Longstreet came to our rescue before any harm came to me or Mrs. O'Rourke."

Tobias returned to serve steaming cups of coffee from a silver tray.

"That will be all, for now, Tobias."

He nodded and removed himself to stand by the door.

Crook picked up his cup. "Have you any idea why Stephen Atkins may have wanted you killed?"

"Stephen? Heavens no. I scarcely knew him. What makes you think he put them up to such a despicable errand?"

"We're only trying to make some connection between Atkins and El Anillo. Did you overhear any discussion of him before the Spaniard Esteban left?"

"No. Why?"

"Esteban left here and traveled to Topeka."

"And that makes him Atkins's killer?"

"That and Atkins's ring finger."

"Ring finger? I'm afraid I don't follow you."

"It was missing, signature of an El Anillo killing."

"How gruesome. Still, I don't see what any of this has to do with me. A man like Atkins must have had any number of enemies. Why, only recently there was that dreadful ruckus over the Royal Gorge right-of-way."

"We've considered that possibility, but we cleared William Palmer of suspicion. We understand you hold a rather substantial interest in the Denver & Rio Grande. That gave you a stake in the dispute."

"I hold a great many investments. Fortunately, the courts settled that dispute in our favor."

"Something or someone brought the ring to bear on killing both of you. You for some good fortune were spared, while Atkins missed his chance at fortune. Curious, don't you think? And cause of some concern for your safety."

"I appreciate your concern. I assure you where my safety is concerned, Tobias is quite competent. Now, if you gentlemen will excuse me, I believe I've taken up enough of your time. Tobias will show you out."

Tobias held the door.

The carriage wheeled away down the road back to Denver as large drops of rain splattered the bonnet.

"What do you make of it?" Cane asked.

"Clever bastard. I'll give him that."

"He didn't give us anything."

"He didn't say anything to tamp down my suspicion either. There's more here somewhere."

"You're probably right. We just can't prove it."

"Yet."

CHAPTER FORTY-FOUR

Denver

Longstreet sat at his desk haloed in lamplight. He'd taken to working late. When the office cleared out, he had time to think without the painful surroundings at O'Rourke House. *Time, how much would it take?* He'd considered the hope she might return to her senses and come back. After reflecting further on that prospect, he'd concluded the notion wishful foolishness. There was a finality in selling the house. She'd taken pains to leave no hint of her intentions. No trace of a chance he might follow her, find her, and impose on her feelings for him. Feelings for him. Feelings she didn't trust herself to feel. Hope? Not unless Maddie made the first move.

A rap at the door startled the silence. Who could that be at this hour? He rose and made his way up the aisle to the front door. A dark female figure stood silhouetted outside.

He unlocked the door.

"Working late? I've never known you to be so diligent."

"Samantha, what are you doing here?"

"Walking back to the Palace. I saw the light on. Imagine my surprise when I saw an old friend. I should have thought you'd be home with Maddie by now."

Pain pinched his expression.

"Uh-oh. Trouble?"

He stared off into the night.

"Sometimes it helps to talk about things. Walk a girl to her

235

hotel and have some supper. I'm a good listener."

"Let me blow out the lamp."

She took his arm for the short walk to the Palace. They were shown to the quiet table Beau requested in the dining room. He ordered a bottle of sherry. The waiter left them to their menus. Samantha poured, handed Beau his glass, and sat quietly.

"She left."

"She left?"

"Sold the house to Mrs. Fitzwalter and left."

"Why?"

"She said she couldn't marry me for the risks we take in this line of work. I told her I'd give it up. She said she'd not ask that of me. Don Victor kidnapped her to get back at me for killing Escobar. It scared her."

"Can't blame her for that. Most women aren't prepared for that sort of thing."

"There are other ways to make a living."

"There are. You don't strike me as store clerk material though. Maddie must have seen that too. Giving up what you do and living with the decision might be two different things. Did you ever stop to think maybe she knew you better than you know yourself?"

The waiter arrived; two menus unopened. Steaks made it easy. Beau poured another round.

"You could be right. I wasn't much in the making of marriageable material before she came along."

"As I recall all her house rules, neither was she. You broke her rules."

"I did. I didn't do it alone."

"I'm sure you didn't. The kidnapping surely shook her. Sometimes people retreat into themselves in the aftermath of something like that. You represented things she hadn't been comfortable with for quite some time. She's already been widowed once. Confronting the danger you live with held up a future that frightened her."

"She said as much in her letter."

Steaks arrived. Sherries freshened.

"I'm sure this hurts, Beau. In hindsight you may find it for the best. Maddie's rules broke hard for her. You struggled to make a marriage commitment. Marriage may not have been right for either of you."

"I suppose you could be right."

"Beau, it's Samantha."

"It is." He drained his glass and refilled hers.

"You know I kind of miss the old Beau Longstreet. You remember him." She lowered her lashes. "The one who never let a lady . . . down."

"Hmm, I do remember something of him."

"I'm glad to hear that of him." She smiled. "Perhaps we should celebrate his return. First though, we must do something about your tie."

"Is it in need of straightening?"

"Desperately so. I don't believe it can easily be fixed. I think we shall have to take it off and start over. Come along now." She rose and took his hand. "I think there's a good chance we may have the right of it by morning."

Morning sun brightened the room. Longstreet roused to Samantha nibbling his lower lip. He nibbled back. Violet eyes glistened through a curtain of tossed black curls.

"There he is, the old Beau Longstreet," she breathed.

"I always knew there was more to you than your clever wit."

"I should hope so."

"How long do you plan on staying in Denver?"

"Chicago beckons. I've been cooling my heels in Pueblo since the war ended. If I stay away much longer, they'll forget who I am."

"I hardly think that possible."

"Such a sweet boy. Besides, you must have some vital case to work on."

"The Atkins murder. We pretty well know who the assassin is. He left his El Anillo signature."

"I thought you got the Don."

"We did. We think the snake has grown a new head. It's where he's gone we don't know. And without him, we can't lay a finger on our suspect who ordered the killing."

"If you have a suspect you must have a motive."

"Eli Chorus. Ever hear of him?"

"The financier. What makes you think he was behind the murder?"

"Owns a big block of D&RG stock. He had a stake in the Royal Gorge war."

"Really." She knit her brow. "There may be another way to get at him."

"What's that?"

"Paddy O'Cairn."

"The Knights of Labor organizer?"

"That's him. It's only a hunch, mind you, but something he said might fit. When I asked him why strike the AT&S and why now, he said 'Powerful people are willing to pay,' "

"You mean someone put the Knights up to the strike?"

"That's what he said. Then he clammed up tight. Chorus had motive and money."

"And access. His estate is just up the road from Pueblo. Where is O'Cairn now?"

She smiled. "Said he was headed for Chicago."

"Then all we have to do is find the nearest strike."

"Mm-hmm, first chance we get." She nibbled.

CHAPTER FORTY-FIVE

League Office

Longstreet straggled in later than usual that morning. Crook speared him in the doorway with a scowl.

"Midnight oil, midmorning hours, what's to be made of you, Beau?"

"Possible break in the Atkins case."

"Come in, I'm all ears."

"Samantha Maples stopped in last night."

"Does Reggie know?"

"Probably not. She just happened to be passing by."

"Stopped to cheer you up, did she?"

"We had supper."

"So, what did she have on the Atkins case?"

"Only a hunch, but it seems to fit. She worked the Royal Gorge war playing water girl to the AT&S strikers. She got to know the Knights of Labor organizer, one Paddy O'Cairn. When she asked him why the AT&S and why now, he told her 'Powerful people were willing to pay.' "

"Chorus."

"Could be. That might explain an assassination targeting him."

"Ordered by Atkins if he knew Chorus was behind his labor troubles."

"That fits. Chorus buys out his contract in return for one on Atkins."

239

"Which explains what Atkins was doing meeting an El Anillo assassin in a locomotive barn in the middle of the night."

"Unfinished business finished him."

"Where is this O'Cairn chap now?"

"Sam thinks Chicago."

"Sounds like you should pack."

"Will do."

"Did she?"

"Did she what?"

"Cheer you up?"

Longstreet smiled.

"Nice to have you back."

Cheyenne

The Denver stage wheeled west on Sixteenth Street. The driver hauled lines at the station two blocks from the depot. Longstreet stepped down and offered Samantha his hand. Wind gusted out of the west, hot and dry, running cotton-ball clouds over a bright blue sky. They waited on the boardwalk for luggage to be unloaded from the boot. Longstreet gathered both valises.

"U.P. Hotel for old times' sake?" he asked.

"My, my, have we gone sentimental too?"

"No need to tiptoe around Sir Reggie this time."

"There is that."

"One room or two?"

"Don't be silly."

"Just checking. Don't wish to presume."

"Just give me time for a bath after two days in that four-wheeled torture chamber."

"I'll find the bar. You can find me there."

Fresh as a flower, scented in lilac. A lavender gown replacing traveling weeds. Samantha swept into the lounge, turning heads.

240

Longstreet nursed a beer at a corner table absorbed in a newspaper.

"Hi, handsome. Buy a girl a drink?"

Longstreet rose to hold her chair and signal the bartender.

Portly with a thin layer of slick hair and a white apron the bartender waddled to the table. "What'll it be?"

"Sherry," Samantha said.

"Make it two." Longstreet took his seat. "Feeling better?"

"Much. Find anything interesting?" she nodded to the paper.

"No reports of labor unrest in Chicago, so no."

"O'Cairn shouldn't be that hard to track down. I suspect the Knights have an office there."

"That would be convenient."

"Do you think he'll cooperate?"

"Do you? You know him. I don't."

"Not willingly. He was pretty protective of whoever paid them off."

"About what I figured."

"So what will you do?"

"Lie."

"Of course. Why didn't I think of that?"

"You would have, given time to think about it."

The bartender arrived with their drinks. Samantha lifted her glass.

"So much for business."

Longstreet touched his glass to hers, "So much."

Chicago

The Knights of Labor occupied a renovated warehouse in an aromatic part of town east of the stockyards. Longstreet took up watch. He didn't have long to wait before a man fitting Samantha's description of O'Cairn made an appearance. From there Beau followed him to a working man's pub a short walk from the office. Inside, the dimly lit dark smelled of stale tobacco, beer, and sweat. He spotted his man at the bar and sidled up to him.

"O'Cairn."

He lifted a brow. "Do I know you?"

"Not directly. Eli Chorus suggested you might be able to help me."

O'Cairn turned, his eyes fixed on Longstreet. "Never heard of him."

"He said you could be retained to arrange a labor problem."

"Don't know what you're talking about. Tell you what I do know, though. I can smell Pinkerton a mile away."

"I'm not a Pinkerton."

"You say. I see. Your bruisers follow us wherever we go." He turned back to his beer.

"Would it trouble you to know Chorus is implicated in a murder investigation?"

"No."

"The victim was Stephen Atkins."

"The railroad baron?"

"The same."

"Got what he deserved. Too bad nobody took it to Palmer for callin' you bastards down on us. I've heard enough of your bullshit. Now I'm gonna sit down with some of my friends. They may not appreciate you fouling the air in here. If I was you, I'd get myself gone."

Palmer House

Samantha added style to the gilded lobby surroundings. She spied Longstreet waiting in a green-velvet wing chair.

"Sorry I'm running a little late. Duty presses."

"No matter. You're here." He offered his arm. "You look like you could use a drink."

She smiled.

The salon was quiet. Elegantly appointed the guests conversed in genteel understated tones. Longstreet selected a table. "Sherry?"

"Bourbon."

"Tough day at the office?"

She offered a half-lidded smile. "Freshens the appetites."

"Two bourbons it is then." He signaled the waiter.

"So, how did it go with O'Cairn?"

"Not as well as I'd hoped."

"Tell me about your lie."

"I pretended Chorus sent me."

"Interesting."

"Not really. He claimed he'd never heard of him."

The waiter arrived in a starched white jacket bearing their drinks on a silver tray.

They toasted.

"You'll love the next part. He said he could smell Pinkerton a mile away."

She gave a throaty laugh. "What, and you couldn't explain that away with your Great Western Detective League cover?"

"Didn't see much point in trying that. Squeezed him with Chorus being implicated in the Atkins murder investigation. It meant nothing to him other than Atkins probably got what he deserved."

"So where does that leave you?"

"Another layer of suspicion on Chorus, but no proof. I expect the Colonel will call us off the case until the Spaniard surfaces or Chorus makes another move."

"The ring has more lives than a cat."

"Seems so."

"At least there's a bright side to all this."

"What's that?"

"You're in Chicago and so am I."

"There is that, isn't there."

"How long can you stay?"

"I'll work at it for a while."

"I was hoping you would."

"Let's have some supper while the appetite's fresh."

CHAPTER FORTY-SIX

O'Rourke House
Denver, 1910

Cane paused. I put my pencil aside, resting my writer's cramp. A golden glow turned the parlor a mottled sepia hue filtered through tree-lined shadows. Afternoon faded toward evening. Our time must necessarily come to an end.

"Presumably Longstreet made it back to Denver."

"Eventually."

"And the Colonel?"

"Called us off the case as expected. Nothing further could be done pending some new development."

"So ends the case of the Assassin's Witness."

"We can't claim it came to a fully fruitful conclusion, though we did avert total war at the Royal Gorge and put an end to Don Victor and one of his henchmen."

Angela appeared in the foyer. "Oh, Robert, we've received our invitation. We shall be more than delighted to attend your wedding."

"Splendid. Penny will be so pleased."

"And you may tell her for me she did."

I sensed my brows knit. "Did what?"

"Tasteful elegance."

"Tasteful elegance, I'm not sure I understand."

"The invitation. She said she'd know it when she saw it. Well, she did."

245

"I shall tell her." Tasteful elegance, I'd forgotten. I made a mental note to have another look at the invitations. I'd licked the envelopes. Tasteful never entered into it, let alone elegance. I rose. "Well, I shall leave you two to your evening. I'm to meet Penny for supper." Angela showed me out.

She returned to the parlor. "Such a nice young man. Young Penny is fortunate to have captured his heart."

"I might suppose it the other way around. A fortunate man who makes a good match."

"I'm surprised you should notice such a thing."

He patted the settee beside him. "Come now, am I so disagreeable a curmudgeon?"

She took her seat. "Hmm, I shall have to consider that."

"I'll have you know I've come to consider you . . ."

"Groping for the word?"

"Agreeable. That's it. Most agreeable."

"Agreeable! What sort of sentiment is that?"

"Comfortably agreeable."

"You make it sound like an old slipper."

"Oh, you know what I mean."

"I most assuredly do not . . ." *intend to let you off the hook so easily.*

"It's only I, a man of few words."

"Now it's words he says."

He wrapped her in a tender hug and a gentle kiss. "Better?"

"Better than an old slipper."

"I should hope. Agreeable too."

Holy Redeemer Episcopal Church
June 12, 1910
The long-awaited day dawned bright and sunny with the barest hint of mountain breeze to cool the heat of the day. I arrived at the church as appointed, agitated by nervous expectations I

hadn't anticipated. I surmised it was the enormity of the step we were about to take, though after all the courtship, care, and planning the occasion surely should not have come as a surprise. I met Father Taylor in the sacristy. He endeavored to calm me with assurances my feelings of nervousness were quite normal.

We waited in a soft stained-glass glow scented in wood polish and candle wax as the guests arrived to take places in the pews. As I watched, I felt the Colonel's presence. I imagined the old curmudgeon managed a smile as he witnessed fruition come to all the mischief his teasing had wrought. I wondered if Penny might sense him too. I made a mental note to ask her after the ceremony. I'd ask my new wife. It seemed a fitting first question for her.

We hadn't invited a large party of guests. A few of Penny's associates at Shady Grove, the receptionist who regaled me with her knowing looks and smiles among them. A like number of my colleagues from the *Tribune* were also in attendance. Briscoe was there of course in the company of Angela, more betwixt them I suspected than met the eye. They were joined in their pew by an older couple I did not recognize. Some relative of my Penny I supposed.

At the appointed hour, Mrs. Taylor struck up the organ with the familiar first chords of the traditional Wedding March. Father Taylor led me out to the altar at the head of the center aisle to await my bride. She appeared in the entrance at the back of the church. My apprehensions melted in a vision of white. The dress was simple, delicate, and elegant at once. A lace veil muted the glow of her eyes and her smile. She started up the aisle in measured steps. Heads turned. I watched Angela smile and nod. She approved the dress, I wagered. Penny would be pleased.

The bright spray of columbine she carried just below her waist rested on a lovely bed of yarrow. Columbine, I rolled the symbolism around my bedazzled brain. The goddess of love struck me as perfect as the moment. As she reached the altar, I put the thought aside for later, though I must admit, not too far aside.

Penny's caramel eyes glistened beneath her veil. She smiled. I took her hand. We exchanged a private squeeze and turned to Father Taylor.

"Dearly beloved, we are gathered here today to unite this man and this woman in the holy state of matrimony."

The familiar lines ran on . . . for richer, for poorer . . . in sickness and in health . . . until death do us part.

We exchanged our "I do's," kissed, and celebrated the solemnity of an ancient sacred ritual. Father Taylor celebrated our union before our guests, counseling us on the virtues and trials of married life while lavishing our love for one another in high praise. I confess parts of it may have reddened my cheeks and tightened my collar. For her part Penny moistened an eye. The service felt a proper start to our new life together.

When at last the organ announced our time to depart, Penny took my arm as we made our way down the aisle to the smiles and approving nods of our guests.

A carriage waited outside the church to whisk us away to the Palace Hotel in a shower of rice and good wishes. I recall picking Briscoe up in the crowd along with the gentleman I'd not recognized in church. There seemed something oddly familiar about him, much in the same manner I'd subconsciously recognized Briscoe at the Colonel's graveside. I must confess I gave it no more thought than a mental note to ask Briscoe about him when next we met. At the moment I found myself taken with more pressing excitement.

With that I shall close this chapter in our story by simply saying, our columbine were well chosen.

★ ★ ★ ★ ★

"So that's the author," Longstreet said.

" 'Tis," Briscoe nodded.

"I shall have to meet him sometime."

"You should. Nice young fellow. Seems to have a flair for our adventures."

"He does. The Sam Bass case first caught my eye. Not much of a reader, but I remembered that case. Couldn't believe what I found when I opened the book to my part in all of it. You say the Colonel put him up to it."

"Not exactly. Robert stumbled on the idea in newspaper archives. Can't believe folks read newspapers much less old newspapers, but he did. Found the Colonel up at Shady Grove and for the price of a bottle of whiskey, well, you know the rest."

"Speaking of whiskey."

"We should."

"The ladies?"

"Angela's been known to."

"Mine too."

"Let's do then."

ABOUT THE AUTHOR

Paul Colt's critically acclaimed historical fiction crackles with authenticity. His analytical insight, investigative research, and genuine horse-sense bring history to life. His characters walk off the pages of history in a style that blends Jeff Shaara's historical dramatizations with Robert B. Parker's gritty dialogue. Paul does Action Adventure, western style. Paul's *Grasshoppers in Summer* received Finalist recognition in the Western Writers of America Spur Awards. *Boots and Saddles: A Call to Glory* received the Marilyn Brown Novel Award, presented by Utah Valley University. Readers say, *"Pick up a Paul Colt book, you can't put it down."* To learn more visit Facebook @paulcoltauthor

The employees of Five Star Publishing hope you have enjoyed this book.

Our Five Star novels explore little-known chapters from America's history, stories told from unique perspectives that will entertain a broad range of readers.

Other Five Star books are available at your local library, bookstore, all major book distributors, and directly from Five Star/Gale.

Connect with Five Star Publishing

Visit us on Facebook:
https://www.facebook.com/FiveStarCengage

Email:
FiveStar@cengage.com

For information about titles and placing orders:
(800) 223-1244
gale.orders@cengage.com

To share your comments, write to us:
Five Star Publishing
Attn: Publisher
10 Water St., Suite 310
Waterville, ME 04901